BAD BLOOD

Cora's Choice – Book 3

V. M. BLACK

D1519779

Aethereal Bonds
aetherealbonds.com

Swift River Media Group
Washington, D.C.

ISBN: 1500868477
ISBN-13: 978-1500868475

FICTION / General
FICTION / Coming of Age
FICTION / Fantasy / Urban
FICTION / Gothic
FICTION / Political
FICTION / Romance / General
FICTION / Romance / New Adult
FICTION / Romance / Paranormal
FICTION / Thrillers / Supernatural
FICTION / Thrillers / Political

ALONE WITH THE VAMPIRE

MY LIPS FORMED HIS NAME. *"Dorian."*

He gave a broken chuckle. "The world falling down around our ears, and what I want most is…you." He lowered his face to mine. "To take you."

He was so close to me. My hand shifted, no longer hooked over his but gripping his forearm. Little tremors of arousal shivered down into me.

"Take me," I breathed, an echo, an invitation—and a dare.

And then his lips met mine, and nothing else mattered. The world and all its horrors and complications fell away, and there was only him, his body, long and lean against mine, his mouth over mine, laying claim to it like he had laid claim to my body and my life.

Heat unfurled inside me, wakened by the electric tingle that went from his lips down to the juncture of my thighs. I pressed myself against him, opening my mouth to him, wanting him more than anything as I stood in front of the very doors through which I'd tried to escape him only the day before.

He pulled back.

"Dammit, Cora," he said roughly. "The blood—all that blood. In the vehicle, I had almost…." A shudder went through his body. It passed from his to mine, the sudden violence of his desire sweeping across me as some invisible control that he had clamped over it suddenly loosed, broken.

Aethereal Bonds

aetherealbonds.com

Cora's Choice

Life Blood
Blood Born
Bad Blood
Blood Rites
Blood Bond
Blood Price

The Alpha's Captive

Taken
Pursuit
Flight
Haven
Escape
Freed

ACKNOWLEDGEMENTS

To my readers, who make this all possible

CONTENTS

CHAPTER ONE

I got out of the dead car and stepped into the biting winter night. My stomach was knotting so hard I had to force myself to stand up straight, shivers wracking my body even as I turned to face down the three SUVs that came bouncing up the dirt road toward me.

My hunters.

I wasn't going to escape them this time.

I held my ground. It wasn't bravery—there was just nowhere else to go. I was out of gas and out of luck. My belly roiled with cold and terror, but I tipped my chin up, determined not to give them the satisfaction of seeing my fear.

The SUVs stopped a dozen yards away. The idling

of their engines was the only sound I could hear above the chattering of my teeth.

A man emerged from the driver's side of the middle vehicle. His wide shoulders were thrown into silhouette by the blazing headlights as he closed in on me.

The people who had been chasing me all day had won. I didn't know who they were, and I didn't know why they wanted me dead, but they were going to get their way.

It was stupid. *I* was stupid. I'd gone half crazy, trying to figure out how I was going to live in the new world that had been thrust upon me when the answer was simple. I wasn't going to live at all.

But I wouldn't go down without a fight. Staring down the approaching man, I formed a fist around my keys, the only weapon I had. The cards on the keychain cut into my palm as I forced the ends of the keys to stand out in points between my fingers.

"Hello, Cora. Merry Christmas."

The words shot through me with a force that rocked me on my feet. I recognized that voice, and instantly afterward, I recognized the presence, the one that I'd been too terrified to sense. Not my attackers.

Dorian Thorne. The vampire.

He'd come to get me.

I heard a sound, a cry, and I realized that it was mine. I ran forward, half-stumbling with cold, flinging myself against his chest. His heady influence enveloped me like a drug, the darkness of him taking my breath away, even now.

My savior. My fate.

It was all his fault. The only possible motivation anyone had for coming after me was my connection to Dorian. And he hadn't warned me, much less protected me.

"You bastard!" The insult tore from my throat. "You absolute prick!"

I hauled my hand back—the one without the keys still clenched in it—and hit him with all of my strength. He made no move to avoid it, didn't catch my hand even though I knew that it would be trivial to his vampire-fast reflexes, nor did he flinch when I made contact with his beautiful cheekbone.

Dorian simply took the strike, then wrapped his arms around me even as I kicked and struggled, holding me against him as I worked out my fear and fury, screaming out at him, at my attacker, and at the world that had driven me to this desolate, freezing road and nearly to my death.

"You're safe now," he said. "I have you, and you are safe."

I had the sense that he was trying to convince himself of the truth of those words as much as he was reassuring me.

The burst of adrenaline-fueled energy left as quickly as it had come, wringing the last strength from me. I went limp, hanging from his hold, shivering taking control of my body again even as I panted with effort.

"Safe? You're the one who nearly got me killed," I said. "I was going to die, and it was your fault."

And now here I was, back in his grasp in a quite literal way. Safe from my pursuers, perhaps—but not safe from him.

He was the one enemy that I didn't even have the will to fight—the one I couldn't even name an enemy without a pang that said that I was wrong, wrong, wrong. I'd only been able to want to strike him because he let me.

Dorian lifted me effortlessly into his arms. I made a faint protest. But his chest was solid, a certainty amid the day's chaos and confusion. Safe and certain, the way a prison's bars were….

"I know," he said, carrying me toward the second of the three long black Escalades that were idling on the dirt road.

"You were supposed to save me." It was a stupid and illogical protest—what did cancer have to do with inhuman attackers?—but it was true. Everything that had happened in the last week had been because he had promised a cure to the cancer that was killing me.

He had delivered on that promise—at least as far as I could tell. But he hadn't told me that the cure would work by changing me into something not-quite-human or that it would blood-bond me to him forever. Not that I would have changed my mind about it, since my alternative was death.

But there didn't seem to be much of a point in my cure if my new connection to him would paint a target on my back. Dead was dead, whether it was from cancer or a murderer.

"I know. Believe me, Cora, I know."

Dorian's voice was full of suppressed force, a cold

fury that rolled off him in waves. I looked up at his face, really looked, and I saw lines of worry carved deep into his unnaturally perfect features.

He had been scared, I realized with abrupt clarity. He had been almost as scared as I was.

Scared of losing me.

He ducked to set me in the passenger's seat before I had time to process that realization. The leather was so deliciously warm against my frozen body that I couldn't even summon horror at the thought of my bloodied shirt pressed between me and the seat.

I knew he wanted me. Needed my body and my blood. For my part, it was impossible to resist his attraction—his vampiric influence meant that any merely human scruples went out the window as soon as he turned the force of his will on me.

I craved him because I must. But did the idea of losing him frighten me?

I wasn't sure.

"Let me see your injury," Dorian ordered.

Of course he'd noticed it. He noticed everything.

"It's healed already," I said, but I had no choice. Shoving my keys in my pocket, I turned in the seat so that my back faced the open door.

Dorian's hands on my back sent tendrils of heat curling through me even in my half-frozen state. He carefully pushed the shredded remains of my hoodie and t-shirt up my back, sliding his hands across the smooth skin beneath.

I knew what he saw there: faint silvery marks, the only evidence of how the creature's claws had slashed me in the attack. Any human would have needed to seek medical attention immediately after such a wound.

Lucky for me, I wasn't fully human anymore.

"She ruined my hoodie," I muttered. "It was my favorite. And probably my pants, too, and I've had these since high school."

"I will buy you another," Dorian said flatly.

"I'm not four years old. I don't want another. I liked this one."

Unaccountably, I felt tears prick my eyes. I hadn't cried once the entire time I thought I was going to die, but now, at the thought that my UMD hoodie was shredded beyond repair, I had to clear my throat and blink hard several times.

Stupid.

Dorian pulled the edge of my shirt down again. He hooked an arm around my chest for a moment and pressed a kiss into my hair. I leaned back against him, closing my eyes, my body wakening to his touch.

"I will not lose you now."

His words were so soft that I thought for a moment I might have imagined them. Then he stepped away and swung my door shut. Bonelessly, I sank back against the seat, wishing that he hadn't let me go.

Wishing I were truly free.

Dorian circled around in front of the headlights to swing into the driver's seat beside me. There was, I noticed, some kind of short shotgun strapped to the console between the seats.

"My car," I said weakly as Dorian put the vehicle into gear. My Gramma had given me her Focus when I got my first off-campus job in college. I couldn't just abandon it, even if it had probably been totaled in my escape.

"I will send someone for it."

The other two SUVs started moving, echoing Dorian's flawless three-point turn that got us facing back the other way.

Back toward D.C.

"I'm not sorry I hit you," I said as I buckled my seatbelt. "You're the reason that…thing tried to kill me. You have to be."

"I am sure I deserved worse." There was no hint of irony in Dorian's voice.

I studied his profile, high forehead and aristocratic nose balanced by a long jaw. His expression was unreadable.

I said, "I thought I was a goner when I realized I'd lost my phone. How did you find me?"

His eyes were fixed to the bumper of the SUV in front of us, the elegant planes of his face thrown into high relief by the light of the reflected high beams. "I had a GPS tracker installed on your car. As a precaution."

"Oh," I said. Because that was totally a healthy, non-stalker-y thing for him to do.

I considered objecting to the invasion of my privacy, but under the circumstances, I decided I couldn't really get upset about it. Whatever his reasons, he'd been proven right.

But I realized I'd expected him to explain he'd found me through some kind of vampiric superpower.

The reality was somewhat anticlimactic.

"It will be months or years before our bond is refined enough that I will be able to use my sense of your distress alone to locate you," he added.

Well, then. "You just let me know when that happens," I said. Because I needed an even bigger case of the screaming meemies around him. "So who the hell just tried to kill me?"

"I don't know." He seemed more tightly contained than he usually was, the intoxicating influence of his presence extending only a few inches from his body. It seemed thicker, though, dark and seething. The thought of touching him like that frightened me.

Scared or not, I wasn't willing to let his answer go. "Seriously. You have so many enemies that you can't even hazard a guess about who would want to kill your—your—" I didn't even know what the word was for a once-entirely-human who had been changed by bonding to a vampire.

"Cognate."

"What?"

"We call you a 'cognate.'"

"Fine, your cognate," I said.

"Yes. Unfortunately, I do have that many enemies," he said calmly. "And so do you, though you should be inviolable to most. And not one of whom should have even known that you exist. Not yet."

The sounds of a muted exchange behind me made my gaze flick up to the rearview mirror. We weren't alone in the car. There were four hulking silhouettes in the middle and back rows of the SUV. At least one of those men exuded a variation of the sensation that I had always associated with Dorian. Another vampire. And I suspected that the other vehicles each had their own squad of heavies inside.

So Dorian had been able to assemble this group in a matter of minutes to come riding to my rescue. Which meant that he'd been expecting trouble, or at least had prepared for it.

That realization was hardly reassuring.

"If you can't say who, then how about what? What was the creature that attacked me?" I asked. It didn't even occur to me that he might not know.

"A djinn."

"Gin," I repeated blankly. "What?"

"Another word for them is genie—but no, not like you're thinking." His voice was calm, reasonable, as if he weren't discussing made-up things. "A djinn is much more like what you imagine a demon might be in your popular culture. They are very strong—stronger even than a single vampire, though not as fast, so they frequently hire themselves out as mercenaries."

My look must have still been incredulous. All I could think of was Disney's *Aladdin* and the *I Dream of Jeannie* reruns I'd seen once when I was sick. But he shook his head.

"You know the kind of child who likes to pull the wings off flies? Who burns ants with a magnifying glass just to see them writhe? That's your average djinn, but with people. No bottles. No wishes. If they were human, you'd call them psychopaths."

"So she was hired to kill me," I said slowly as the

front SUV in our motorcade led the way back onto a paved road.

"Yes."

I shuddered. "I guess it's a good thing whoever it was chose someone who liked to do their work up close. If they'd hired a man with a gun, I wouldn't be here now."

"Habit. Vampires tend not to trust bullets as more than a deterrent. They're good at slowing us down, but unless the shot is perfect, they aren't entirely reliable with our kind." He shrugged. "Or maybe the orders were to kidnap you if possible and kill you if not. She wasn't specific, and we didn't ask."

"You don't know who hired her?"

"According to my friend Clarissa, she didn't know. It was an anonymous transaction."

"You trust her answer?"

"She wasn't in a position to lie." The words had a decisive finality about them.

I rubbed my wrist, where the tiny teardrop-shaped bond mark stood out against the skin. For a moment, I felt a tiny bit sorry for her.

Yeah, only a tiny bit.

The radio bolted onto the vehicle's dashboard crackled to life, interrupting my thoughts.

"Mr. Thorne, it looks like we have a problem here."

Chapter Two

Dorian grabbed the handset. "What is it?"

"Scouts are reporting a roadblock."

"Aethers?"

"Police."

"The police," I said urgently. "They were possessed or something. They tried to shoot me."

Dorian nodded curtly. "I thought Etienne had sorted that," he said into the handset.

"He dealt with the department. These must be puppets."

His jaw flexed, annoyance flashing in his eyes. "Right, everybody. You know what to do."

He hung up the handset with a decisive click and flicked off the headlights, dropping back slightly to let the rear SUV pass.

"*I* don't know what to do," I said.

He didn't look at me as he jerked the quick-releases that held the gun to the console between us. "Can you shoot?"

"No," I said. "I mean, if I guess if I had to—"

"Then don't worry about it," he said tersely, pulling the gun free.

Behind me, I heard hard, metallic noises as the other men in the car readied their weapons.

"I thought that bullets didn't work," I said weakly. My unnaturally sensitive vision had adjusted to the darkness quickly, but I could see no sign of a roadblock, only the bouncing red taillights of the vehicle in front of us.

"Oh, they work well enough," he said, shifting the shotgun's pistol grip to his left hand. "The effects just aren't often permanent—unless the opponent is human, which these seem to be."

The radio spit and crackled again. "Thirty seconds."

Dorian raised an eyebrow at me. "Can you answer that?"

I blinked, then scrabbled at the radio handset. My fingers found the button. "Uh, got that."

"Fifteen seconds." I could see lights ahead now, blue and red, bouncing off the landscape and into the night, but I still couldn't see the cars themselves past the bulk of the SUV directly in front of us.

"Got it," I said again.

"Put it back," Dorian said. "And hold on."

I fumbled to hang up the handset, then grabbed the edges of the seat with both hands as Dorian took a hard right off the road. I braced as the SUV dipped down into a shallow culvert and went grinding up the opposite slope and into the open field. The car bobbed and swayed as it ran across the furrows, jerking me against my belt.

Dorian jerked the wheel again, and now we were running in the dark parallel to the road with only the glow from the dash breaking the total blackness of the night.

Suddenly, I saw the roadblock out of Dorian's side window, a line of four police cruisers angled across the road with three more behind. In the flashing lights, I could make out the cops hunched behind their cars, pistols and rifles at the ready as the two other SUVs came bearing down on them.

The radio came alive a moment before the first one struck. *"Mark."*

The lead SUV hit the puncture strip across the road without slowing, the tires seemingly unaffected by the sharp spikes. With a squeal of rubber and metal, it barreled into the front line of cruisers, throwing them aside like toys as the cops dove out of the way.

The second SUV jerked off to the left of the road before it hit the strip, circling around the blockade on the opposite side as the first pressed forward. The lead Escalade churned into the back two cruisers, which gave way slowly in a burst of gunfire. A cop fell to the ground as we passed. Someone screamed.

"Oh, my God," I said, looking back.

The lead SUV made it through the roadblock behind us as the second one angled back toward the road ahead of us.

"It's not over yet." Dorian's face was set in taut lines, but his eyes never wavered from the field in front of us.

A tangle of overgrowth blocked our way ahead, and Dorian turned the wheel back toward the road just as half a dozen motorcycles buzzed out of the stand of trees, bearing down on the other SUVs and blocking our only path out.

Dorian hit the window control with the butt end of the shotgun's pistol grip. As the window lowered, he calmly leveled the barrel out of it, toward the bikers. He squeezed the trigger, and the report of the shotgun tore through the night, hitting my eardrums like a solid force.

The shot caught the lead rider in the chest, knocking him off and sending his bike sliding across the asphalt in a shower of white sparks.

I gaped, the scream caught in my throat, but the other bikers came on, pulling pistols from their leather jackets as they closed in on the SUVs.

We bounced onto the road just behind the Escalade that had pushed through the blockade, last in line again. There were more shots, the sharp, short barks of the bikers' guns answered by deeper retorts from the SUVs. Dorian rolled up his window again.

A biker blasted past Dorian's window, then one flew past mine. For an instant, I was looking at his pistol through the window, pointed straight at me. I jerked to the side reflexively, but there was nowhere to go. The gun fired, and a tiny spider web of fractures appeared at the point where it struck the window as the biker was whisked away, but the glass held.

"Bulletproof." I could hardly believe my luck.

"Hardened. Not proofed," Dorian said briefly, yanking the steering wheel to the side to slam into another of the bikers who was attempting to pass. The rider went flying, the mass of the SUV making his body flop like a helpless ragdoll as he spun off into the underbrush.

Three more bikers streaked past, and we passed the crumpled forms of others. I looked in the rearview mirror. They were tailing us now, regrouping as they turned around. The men in the back of the car exchanged a few words. Then, on cue, they rolled down their windows, angling their long, ugly guns behind us. They began to fire, and two more bikers dropped back, struck.

The remaining three slowed then, letting the distance between us grow until they dropped out of sight.

After several long minutes, the men in the back rolled up their windows again, and Dorian flicked back on the headlights and returned his gun to its holder on the console.

I stared at him. He must have been aware of my gaze, but he gave no sign of it.

"What the hell was that all about?"

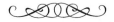

Chapter Three

"They wanted to kill you," Dorian said bluntly. "What part of that would you like explained?"

What I wanted to know about—more than anything—was the casual violence of Dorian's response. How could he point a gun at a human being and pull the trigger with as much thought as I might give to wadding up a piece of scratch paper?

He risked your life with no more thought than that, a part of my brain reminded me. *You, too, could have died when he took your blood, and you would have been just one more dead girl among hundreds.*

I pushed that down, hiding away from myself the lack of revulsion that scared me even more than that thought. I already knew what Dorian would say to them. He'd told me as much before. He wasn't human, and so what he did was never murder. He only killed those that he must in order to live.

"How about the *why*?" I asked instead. "That was an awful lot of trouble to go to—and a lot of blood to spill—if someone just had a grudge against you."

He glanced at me. "It's politics."

"Politics don't usually leave a body count," I countered.

He raised an eyebrow. "How little you know. My enemies, such as they are, disapprove of my research."

That answer took me by surprise. Ancient blood feud, territorial wars, revenge—any of those would have seemed reasonable, at least coming from a vampire. But research?

His research sought to develop medical tests that could better identify potential cognates, humans who were changed by a vampire's bite rather than being killed by it as most were. Those tests had identified me out of thousands, and my bonding to him had been its first clear success.

"Why would anyone object to that?"

"There are many vampires, as you call them, who view humans as cattle, to be used as they see fit."

His blue eyes held me caught in his gaze. Cattle? No, cattle didn't go willingly to the slaughter. But any human caught by a vampire would beg to be bitten by him, even though it almost always meant death.

Including me.

He continued, "But if it takes ten thousand feedings—and ten thousand deaths—to find a cognate, those who put no value on human life will have much support among our people. To hold human life to be important would mean that any feeding that results in death is wrong inasmuch as it can be avoided. And most vampires aren't willing to believe that the very thing that keeps them alive is something that should not occur."

"Okay," I said carefully, suppressing my urge to argue to hear him out. "I get that."

"Now that I can reduce that to one in one hundred—and, most importantly, now that I have proof that I can do it in you—my position becomes much more attractive. Once a vampire has a cognate, no more humans need to die for the length of the cognate's life."

The number of deaths that his moral high road represented was still staggering, but whenever he spoke of it, I felt myself sliding into his way of thinking, like a rock caught in the orbit of the sun.

"And what *is* your position?" I asked. "Equality between humans and vampires?"

The corner of his mouth twitched. "Don't be absurd. But I do hold that humans, like vampires, have unique qualities that make them superior to animals. And that their needless deaths are a waste—and even a crime, if we had such a concept in our society."

I took the words like a blow, though I didn't want to analyze why they hurt. "So when you…approached me, you didn't think I was worth as much as you or any other vampire?"

"If I did, how could I have ever drunk from you? Prolonging my life by four months by taking four months from yours." He shook his head. "A vampire who believed in equality could have only one correct path—to die. And as you see, I am very much alive."

"That's not right," I protested. "It's just not."

"Is it not? You wanted to give. I needed to take. And here you are, alive," he said quietly.

I snapped, "Alive, sure. But now you're—you're claiming that there's something between us, but that only exists because you were willing for me to die. No, that's too nice of a way of putting it. You were willing to kill me. Because you thought my life was that cheap."

"It was that short," he said curtly.

My face felt hot. I wouldn't take that as an answer, not for anything. "And what about now? Is my life worth less than that of a vampire to you now? If that's true, why shoot anyone? Why not just let them take me?"

He glanced over at me, and his pale gaze made me catch my breath. "You aren't human anymore, Cora. You're mine. And you're now worth more to me than any vampire in the world."

That stunned me into a momentary silence, which he used to turn the conversation back to its course.

"They wanted you dead because you're proof that my research works."

I shook my head and regrouped. "You still have the tests, though. Killing me doesn't change that."

"No, it doesn't. But my people believe what they see, and it could take years before we have another success to display even at the new odds. If you could be made to…disappear before you are formally introduced into society, my position would be greatly weakened, perhaps for a decade, perhaps even longer. And a great deal can happen in that time."

"But you let me go home," I said. "You knew there was a danger, and you let me go."

"There shouldn't have been a danger because no one who was not completely loyal to our cause should have known that you existed." His expression was grim. "There is a traitor in our midst—possibly more than one—despite all our safeguards."

"You said you set guards over me. If there wasn't any danger, why would you bother?"

"Because I am a suspicious bastard. It cost me two good men, too." The line of his mouth was bleak.

"Cost you? You mean they're dead?" I felt sick.

I was definitely on board with keeping myself alive, but at what cost? The two guards were unlikely to be the only casualties—at least a few of the motorcyclists who had come after us were probably dead and possibly some of the cops at the blockade, as well.

Worse, there was a good chance that, like the police who had stopped me earlier that day, they weren't even acting of their own free will but were innocents who were manipulated by the vampire who wanted me dead.

You're perfectly willing for other people to die if it will keep you alive. You're not so different from him, after all, are you?

I shuddered at that thought.

"I will provide for their families," Dorian said.

"That doesn't bring them back!"

His gaze flicked over me, and despite everything, I felt the familiar stirring in my center at his gaze. "What else would you have me do, Cora? I can't work miracles. Their murderer has been dealt with, and their families will not want for anything. That is the extent of my powers."

"I don't know," I said weakly. "Maybe don't sound so cavalier."

I should have died that night, in his surgery. Or I should have chosen to accept my cancer as terminal—to go quietly instead of grasping at straws. This is all his fault, but it's mine, too.

"Trust me, Cora. I am anything but cavalier. But this is just the latest skirmish in a very long war, and the stakes are higher than you can imagine."

"I didn't ask for this," I said. I sounded childish. I didn't care.

"I know. And I am sorry." Dorian's look was keen. "This isn't about you, Cora, and it's not your fault. You're just a symbol, a placeholder. It wouldn't matter who was in your place. The battle would still be fought. It must be fought and won."

He sounded more adamant about that than he ever had about anything. A placeholder for them—and a placeholder for him, too, I realized abruptly. He'd been willing to kill the Cora who had walked into his surgery. And now he would kill for me, not because of who I was but because of what he'd made me into.

Did he care about me, Cora Shaw, at all?

Did I even want him to?

He turned back to the road. "If it weren't for the bond still forming, I wouldn't have let you go home at all."

"What do you mean?" I was asking two questions in one—about the bond forming and about his use of the word *let*.

21

"It takes time for the bond to gain its final strength. In the old days, we would stand guard over our cognates as they went through the conversion, and we would keep them as close to us as we could—that's what the bond makes us desire, after all, and we didn't know any better. The bond that formed then was very rigid. To be more than a room or two away would cause the most excruciating pain."

I shivered at the thought of being tied that closely to anyone. *Even Dorian?* came the distant whisper, which made me shiver again.

Dorian didn't seem to notice. "We learned that if we stayed away as much as possible when the bond was fresh, it would become much more flexible when it finished forming. We could be apart for weeks, even, without going mad, or fly half a world away, if needed. A room or two would not even be noticeable. So while you were undergoing your conversion, I stayed in Manhattan until you showed signs of regaining consciousness. For you to return to your own home, resume your old life for at least a day or two after waking would further add to the flexibility. This is why I did not schedule your introduction to society immediately— I chose to wait for the bond to settle."

"Oh," I said in a small voice. "And now?"

"And now that part of the conversion is almost complete."

"That part," I repeated. "And what parts are left?"

"Nothing you need to worry about." He didn't even look away from the road.

Stung, I returned, "I should be the judge of that.

22

You didn't think I had to worry about people trying to kill me, either."

"That's enough, Cora," he said, and the words rippled with his will.

I shut my mouth with a click. I didn't know if he'd force me to stop asking, but I was too much of a coward to find out. How much would he take from me if it meant enough to him that I obey?

But if I didn't ask a question for fear of him forcing me, I was being controlled by him just as surely as if he were messing directly with my head....

"I've just ordered announcements for your introduction to society to be held on Saturday," he continued. "That should end this particular gambit on the part of my enemies, as soon as any remaining puppets are neutralized."

Unable to force myself to grill him about the bond, I put a bite into my next words. "So while I was in mortal danger, you paused to order invitations?"

He ignored my sarcasm. "Not at all. I ordered them while we were tracking you down."

My expression must have revealed my incredulity.

He added, "It was the fastest way to end further threats on your life. And it sent a message to whomever had tried to take you—you must realize that at that moment I fully believed that you were in someone else's power—that I would stop at nothing to get you back."

I believed him. But we'd talk later about the idea of me being introduced—whatever that meant—to a society that largely wanted me dead.

Dorian said, "It is considered out of bounds to attack someone's cognate. We don't have laws, exactly, but we have conventions, a code, that everyone largely follows. Killing a cognate is a precedent that cannot go unpunished. Someone who orders such an attack would be a target for every bonded vampire, and if his associates don't immediately join in the condemnation, they would be targeted, as well. If you could be eliminated before you were introduced to society, however, I would have no proof that you ever existed, so there would be no violation and so no retribution."

"You said my introduction is still two days away," I said. "So does that mean I'll be under fire until then? And what about the cops? As far as the police are concerned, I'm the main suspect in a hit-and-run accident."

"I had the invitation issued in the names of six of the most respected members of our society. Their presence on the invitation vouches for your existence. Unconventional, perhaps, but effective. And the police have already been dealt with. As far as the department is concerned, the incident never happened. The roadblock back there was set in motion many hours ago."

"So are you taking me home now?" I asked. I wasn't sure if I would be more frightened if the answer were yes or no.

"No, Cora. You'll stay in my Georgetown house tonight."

I shivered slightly, remembering what had happened between us the last time I had been in his house. Wanting it to happen again.

Stupid, stupid, stupid....

Dorian didn't notice. "That house is the safest place I have in this country. As for me, I will be staying in Baltimore. Now that I've seen the scale of the attempt, there must be a large Kyrioi-aligned faction behind it—the Star Junta perhaps, or the League of Westphalia. Baltimore is a Kyrioi stronghold and so the best place to track them down."

"Oh," I said, not sure if I was more sorry or relieved that he would be gone and understanding less than half of the rest.

"If you don't want to know any of this, just tell me. Most agnates—that's what vampires call ourselves, you understand—would consider this sort of thing to be beyond your place."

"And what is my place, exactly, then?" I demanded acidly.

He looked amused at my reaction. "Wherever I choose it to be. Right now, your place is eating dinner. Dalton, hand over the basket."

The last order was directed behind us, and I jumped slightly as a basket was passed by one of the men in the middle bench up between the two front chairs.

I hadn't eaten since my late breakfast hours ago. My stomach growled at the smell of the food that wafted from under the cloth cover.

I took it with a somewhat tentative, "Thank you." I pulled off the cloth to discover an assortment of fussy little sandwiches and a thermos underneath. Dorian's chef again, trying to impress me.

I couldn't help it. The stress and fear and exhaustion had been all too much—and now this. Fancy-cut gourmet sandwiches. I burst out laughing.

Dorian raised an eyebrow.

"A picnic fit for a car chase," I said, raising a delicate confection in a salute. "Why not?"

And then I wolfed it down.

The clock on the dash read 10:12 when we pulled up to the front of Dorian's Georgetown house. He threw the SUV into park and circled to my side as one of the men in the back stepped out to take his place in the driver's seat.

My hand was on the door handle when he opened it for me, catching my arm and supporting me as I slid to the ground. At his touch, the trickle of awareness in his presence turned into a sudden flood of raw need, no buffer left in my exhaustion. I half-lurched against his chest as he steadied me. I was too tired to stop myself. I almost despaired to realize that nothing that had happened that day had changed it.

I was frightened at the thought that nothing at all could.

My shredded, bloodied shirt had finally finished drying against the warm captain's chair, and it stuck to my skin and clumped in my ponytail. My legs were wobbly now that the last of my fear-fueled energy had drained away. But none of that mattered with him.

It occurred to me to wonder if Dorian's gallantry was because I was a woman or because I was human. If I were a human man and he was a female vampire—agnate, I corrected—would our roles still be the same? Was it human or vampire society that made him open doors and stand when I entered the room?

I leaned on Dorian's arm as he escorted me up the walk to his bone-white mansion, its classical symmetry standing in merciless perfection over the garden, with its walls of holly and rigidly trimmed boxwood borders along the paths and flowerbeds. Everything was carefully controlled, any hint of unruliness mercilessly lopped off, as if there was a danger in the least unconformity.

We went up the front steps to the portico. Expecting the butler, I was surprised to see an unfamiliar woman open the door. From the power that rolled out from her and her unnatural beauty, with her flawless ebony skin and her slanting almond eyes, she was vampire, not human.

So, I thought, my brain still muddled with exhaustion. *Some vampires are black.*

I didn't know whether that should be a surprise, since I still didn't know where the hell vampires came from in the first place. All I knew was that they'd never been human, and humans could never become vampires.

"They're assembling in the ballroom," she said without introduction when we stepped inside. She didn't even look at me. "It will be another half hour before they're ready for the proving."

27

She didn't affect me the same way Dorian did. I wondered if it was because she was female or due to some side effect of my bond.

Dorian's mouth pressed very briefly in a hard line before her relaxed into his usual marble impassivity. "Very well. We will be there."

The vampire—agnate—raised her eyebrows. "We?"

Dorian looked down at me. "It's up to you, of course. Do you want to see this?"

I started to say, *Of course,* but I stopped myself. I took nothing as a matter of course with him.

"What is it?" I asked carefully.

"If one of my people was subverted, the proving will reveal it."

"Dammit, Dorian, she's a baby," the female agnate said impatiently. "She doesn't understand what's going on. Send her back to her nursery. You can play with her later."

I bristled. She was right—I didn't understand. But if I got sent upstairs, I never would.

"I want to come with you," I said quietly.

The female agnate just shook her head, looking disgusted.

"Half an hour," she repeated. She took the foyer stairs down to the lower level, where I'd never been before.

I looked up at Dorian. We were alone, for the moment. For the first time since he had come to my rescue. As alone, at least, as we ever were in his house.

My arm was still resting lightly over his, a curiously

old-fashioned gesture. Through the fabric of his sports jacket, I could feel the tension in his body shift in keen awareness of me. A ripple of anticipation went through me.

My lips formed his name. *"Dorian."*

He gave a broken chuckle. "The world falling down around our ears, and what I want most is…you." He lowered his face to mine. "To take you."

He was so close to me. My hand shifted, no longer hooked over his but gripping his forearm. Little tremors of arousal shivered down into me.

"Take me," I breathed, an echo, an invitation—and a dare.

And then his lips met mine, and nothing else mattered. The world and all its horrors and complications fell away, and there was only him, his body, long and lean against mine, his mouth over mine, laying claim to it like he had laid claim to my body and my life.

I knew now what he was even more clearly than before. A killer. Ruthless in pursuit of his goals. Willing to gamble my life to satisfy his thirst—and willing to end a thousand to keep me.

The thought of it should have made me sick, and I knew that later it would. But when it really counted, when I was in his arms, I didn't care about what he was or what he'd done. I couldn't. I needed him too much.

Heat unfurled inside me, wakened by the electric tingle that went from his lips down to the juncture of my thighs. I pressed myself against him, opening my mouth to him, wanting him more than anything as I stood in front of the very doors through which I'd tried to escape him only the day before.

He pulled back.

"Dammit, Cora," he said roughly. "The blood—all that blood. In the vehicle, I had almost…." A shudder went through his body. It passed from his to mine, the sudden violence of his desire sweeping across me as some invisible control that he had clamped over it suddenly loosed, broken.

CHAPTER FOUR

I gave a small, ragged gasp, my skin suddenly alive and burning under his hands, wanting his touch, his mouth, his teeth, his bite—

"You have to get out of those clothes, Cora." The darkness was roiling out of him now in streams that seemed to dim the light. He grabbed me by the upper arm and pulled me in three long steps over to one of the two bronze doors that stood directly off the foyer.

Dazed, I could neither resist nor assist him. He flung the door open, slapping on the light to reveal a row of coats within. He pushed me in ahead of him, then, keeping me at arm's length.

Dorian grabbed my hoodie and the shirt under it and ripped them from collar to seam in one motion. He flung them away, deeper in the closet, and took hold of my bra where the cups met the band. With another quick jerk, the fabric gave, and he threw it after.

I stood, swaying under the force of his regard, a welter of thoughts coming over me that I didn't dare to examine too closely. I didn't want to put a name to my sudden longing—because not only did I want him, but I wanted him to hurt me. He'd been so gentle before, just as he'd promised. I wanted to feel what it would be like when he wasn't—I wanted to feel my finger in the candle flame again.

And the thought scared me almost as much as he did.

His eyes seemed to be holes into another universe, sucking at my soul. He traced a hooked finger along my jaw and down my neck.

"It's still on your skin," he said softly. "In your hair, Cora."

"I know." I breathed the words. My heart was loud in my ears, a terrified thrum, fast and jerky.

Please, please, please....

Then his mouth silenced mine, his body driving me back into the coats, hard against the wall. He rolled my pants down over my hips even as my own shaking hands scrabbled to loosen his belt. My head was heavy and light at once, my limbs tingling with demand.

The hot ache was growing, a slickness between my legs that begged for him. I could smell my need in the confines of the closet, and I could smell him and the metallic tang of my blood.

His hands were rough on my back, tangled in my matted hair, moving down across my breasts, across my belly to find my clitoris. His mouth descended in a line down my jaw and neck, hard against my body, his teeth against my skin, so close to making it part, the hot blood spilling out—

My body was on fire. I shook as I neared my peak, but he didn't give it to me. With a low sound, he turned me in his arms, pushing my face against the cold wall. His hand hooked around my hips drove me onward as his mouth found the bloodied skin of my back.

He pulled my hips back, toward him, even as he pushed up and in, filling me with a sudden motion and surprising a noise from me as he came up against my deepest place. The shudders of his body as he tasted my blood shot through me with every hard stroke.

And I shattered, the hot darkness roaring out from my center, connecting his mouth on me, his hands, his erection deep inside me, my hands clenching around fistfuls of fabric as I cried out. I felt him come seconds later, and then, almost as abruptly, he stepped away, leaving me gasping and leaning against the wall for support.

I rolled against the wall to face him, shaking with the aftermath and with all the thoughts that still tumbled through my head. I could still feel the darkness seething around him. I knew what he had really wanted—to open my veins, to drink from me. To break me, so that I spilled out all at once.

I knew what he wanted because the complimentary urge had burned in my body—the urge to give until nothing was left. He had held back. But I wouldn't have. Even if I were strong enough to fight him, I wouldn't have wanted to. I would have given him everything he'd asked for, and I'd have begged him to take more. No matter what the cost.

I clung to the coats as if they could offer some support.

"Not a good time," he said abruptly. "Too close to bonding. Too much temptation. Too much to lose."

I didn't understand what the time since bonding had to do with anything, but I nodded anyway, my body still trembling with reaction. If it had something to do with what I was feeling, I could only agree.

"Wear this," he ordered, holding out a long woolen coat without looking at me.

Wordlessly, I toed off my tennis shoes so I could strip off my yoga pants and underwear, which were dark red and stiff where the blood of my wounds had run down from my back. I used the leg of the pants to clean myself up quickly, then wrapped the long coat around my body, buttoning it from neck to knee and leaving my blood-matted ponytail tucked inside.

Dorian took a deep breath. I knew he could still smell the blood—I could still smell it, thick and cor-rupted in the air. But now that I was covered and my bloody clothes were far away, he relaxed fractionally and straightened his clothes.

My heart was still beating hard as I put my shoes back on, my limbs weak with the aftereffects of adrena-line. Fear, I realized. That primal part of my body knew exactly what had happened, how close I'd come to an edge I couldn't return from, and I shook with the reac-tion. I fumbled with my laces, getting them tied again somehow.

When I straightened, Dorian stood in the doorway,

his face a mask. He made no attempt to touch me again.

"I am sorry, Cora," he said quietly.

"Don't be," I said. "You stopped." *Don't be, because I wanted more....* My mind reeled away from the thought.

"I will always stop," he said.

He didn't mean that he would not drink my blood. That would happen again. I knew it, and at that moment, I not only accepted it, but I was glad. What he had wanted at that moment went far beyond that. He had wanted me to be opened, to be flayed, to give him everything I had until there was nothing left.

And I would have. I'd heard stories of kinks and fetishes, of dangerous games and safe words.

With a vampire, there was never a safe word. Even to the very end.

"Will you ever stop scaring me?" I asked. But that's not what I really meant. What I really meant was, would I ever stop scaring myself?

A brief, humorless smile flicked over his lips. "I hope not. If I do, then we are both damned."

He stepped out of the coat closet, back into the foyer. "Come on. You're safe now."

Safe. He'd said that word when he had rescued me on the road. Now he meant that I was safe from him.

I took a deep breath and joined him. There was nothing else to do.

"This way," he said, and he led the way across the foyer to another bronze door, the twin of the one he'd just opened.

"Another coat closet?" I asked.

"Not this one," he said, and he swung it open. "I

want to show you something. Before we go down."

The lights were off, but the room glowed from the light of the bank of monitors against the wall. I stared, mesmerized, at the rotating display. The salon, from four different angles. The grounds. What must be a garage. Rooms I recognized—and many more that I did not. My attention was drawn by a huge room in which a crowd of people milled about. It must be the ballroom, I realized.

"They're here for the proving," Dorian said quietly, keeping his distance from me.

"Proving for what?"

"A thrall. To see if any of them has been compromised by another agnate."

Thrall, like enthralled? The police who'd chased me had certainly had something done to their heads.

"You mean like the police? And those bikers?" I asked.

I was pretty sure the motorcyclists had been human, even with their helmets. They'd shown none of the impossible speed or strength of an agnate or a djinn.

"Exactly like that," he said. "A human can be persuaded of a great deal in an agnate's presence. To maintain a deeper level of control, a control that does not dissipate with distance or in another agnate's presence, requires a longer term hold, called a thrall. I hold provings monthly, as much for my staff's protection as for mine. They like the assurance that they can't be made another agnate's agent for months at a time, and the provings mean that other agnates hardly ever even try."

"Hardly ever. That's not the same as never," I said. I looked away from the changing view of the people gathered in the ballroom to frown at Dorian.

He shrugged. "One every few decades. I can't keep them from being subverted, but a proving will break the thrall and enable them to tell me what happened to them and what secrets they betrayed. That makes the technique of limited use to one of my enemies."

"But you suspect that at least one of them is…subverted…now."

His expression was grim. "Not many others, human or agnate, knew of your conversion until you called me for help. If a human is put under another's thrall, he will do the other agnate's bidding until the control is broken—including telling him all about you."

I looked again at the people standing around the room. They looked so ordinary. Some appeared to be my age or even younger. Others looked older than my Gramma. Tall and short, fat and thin. Some were talking in animated groups. Many looked bored. A few looked angry or scared. They didn't look special or different. They could have been any crowd, selected at random.

But they weren't. They were all employees of an ageless vampire. And he'd already told me that they all knew what he was. I was sure that, without compulsion from another agnate, they'd never betray that knowledge. Dorian would never allow that.

The thought made a sour taste in my mouth even as I asked the question.

"So they're all in your thrall, then? Normally, I mean?"

"Of course," he said. "It's a part of the proving, and every agnate must demand absolute loyalty from those who serve him."

His cold logic made the thought no more pleasant.

"Then they aren't ever doing anything of their free will. They're just…puppets," I said, remembering the word that the person on the other end of the radio had said.

"With some agnates, that is the case," he said evenly. "They wish their servants to be nothing more than bodies to do their will. I have found that allowing people to have full lives, both in the physical world and in their own minds, is mutually beneficial. I require only loyalty, nothing more. And those who serve me know this before they make the choice to do so."

"Why would anyone agree to that?" I protested. But I knew. A vampire could make cutting off one's own arm seem attractive in his presence. How many people would even hesitate if he asked only for loyalty?

"There are certain advantages." His tone was dry. "Aside from my charm, which humans find not inconsiderable, I pay well, the job always has complete satisfaction, and there is a lesser version of the benefits that you enjoy—a slightly increased resistance to human ailments and a somewhat decreased rate of aging. There are many humans who would give much to live longer than ordinary people. These benefits are directly related to the closeness of working with us and the frequency of the renewal of the thrall."

"I suppose so," I said, still feeling uncomfortable about the entire idea. "So how do you…put them under your thrall?"

"A small amount of their blood is mixed with mine externally, then taken by mouth," he said. "This establishes a new thrall, replacing any that already exists."

"It doesn't kill them? I mean, when you bite someone—"

"No, saliva doesn't mix in their bloodstream, so it does no harm."

I thought about this for a moment. "And to break a thrall without making a new one?"

"That would be another area of research," he said dryly. "One without a compelling enough benefit to invest in. Even if a human is nominally under an agnate's thrall, it doesn't mean that the agnate must affect him. If the agnate chooses to give him no orders or thoughts, he would not live any differently than a person in no thrall at all. And a thrall fades over time of its own accord. If a vampire desires a true puppet, the thrall should be renewed every week. Even the slightest influence is entirely dissipated within a few years."

"What about a bond?" I asked the question that was more relevant to me. "Can it be broken or reformed with the blood of another vampire? Does it...dissipate?"

His face went perfectly still. "No, Cora. Bonds don't work like that. They never dissipate, and if another agnate tried to feed from you, you would both die."

I wondered if he would lie to me.

But I knew the answer. Of course he would. If the stakes were high enough, he was capable of anything.

Dorian stared fixedly at the monitor that showed

the various views of the ballroom. The crowd was now shuffling into neat lines.

"It's time to go," he said. "Let us hope that we are lucky." He stepped away from the monitors, heading out the door and back into the foyer.

"Lucky?" I echoed.

He cast a look at me back over his shoulder.

"And no one dies."

CHAPTER FIVE

I trailed Dorian down the stairs toward the ball-room, my mind buzzing with questions. He was keeping a careful distance from me now—reducing the temptation that my blood presented to him, I real-ized.

And I was following him. *Really smart, Cora.*

The staircase ended in a grand vestibule, a row of columns dividing it from the vast room beyond. The ballroom itself was a rococo confection in white and gold, the mirrored walls glittering with the light reflected from a dozen chandeliers. There must have been two hundred people gathered on the parquet floor, though the room was so large that it could have held five times as many.

41

The crowd was no longer milling about but was standing in four precise lines fronting a narrow table at the near end of the room where the ballroom met the vestibule. I recognized the butler at the front of one of the lines. That's why he hadn't opened the door—he had to undergo the proving, too, like everyone else.

Three vampires stood behind the table, the female agnate and two others I hadn't seen before, their indolent expressions at odds with the tension their postures betrayed. On the waist-high table was an assortment of medical-looking equipment.

I felt a little queasy.

"Ready?" one of the agnates asked as we stepped into the room. This one was a male—and like the female agnate when she greeted us upstairs, I could sense the force of his will, but it just washed over me, leaving no effect behind.

So the bond did keep them from affecting me. That was good to know. It was bad enough being addled by one vampire—being controlled by any that came along would have been far too much to handle.

Dorian gave a curt nod and stepped up to join them, taking the empty place between two of them so that he stood in front of the last line. I hovered near the stairs, not certain I wanted to be there at all but unable to look away.

"First four, step forward," Dorian ordered the ranks of humans.

The people at the front of the lines stepped up, each to a different vampire. The agnates moved with inhuman speed but not so quickly that I couldn't catch their motions.

First, they pricked the human's finger with a lancet, like those used with glucose monitors. Taking the drop of blood on the end of a fat white pill, they squeezed another drop from a syringe on top of it, mixing the two. Then the human bent down, opened his mouth, and the agnate put the white pill, now stained red with blood, inside.

Red pill or blue pill…. The crazy thought, a movie reference from nowhere, popped into my mind. These people, though, had no choice.

The first four people in line swallowed their pills and stepped aside, making room for the next group at the table as the used lancets were discarded. The butler took up a station to the side of the table with a glower on his face, as if taking the proceedings as a personal insult.

Two of the women who had finished the proving moved to an empty part of the room and began to chat in soft voices, keeping an eye on the action at the proving table. But the last walked quickly past me to the stairs.

"Pardon, madam, my in-laws are watching the kids," she said in explanation when she caught me staring at her for a sign that she had been changed in some way.

I blinked, but she was gone before I could do more than make a strangled sound in reply.

Right. She'd left her in-laws at home on Christmas Day so that her bondage to a deathless vampire could be confirmed.

Why not?

The lines moved quickly. Was the proving even doing anything? I didn't know what to look for, but none of the people seemed to react in any meaningful way. A few of them followed the first woman up the stairs as soon as they took their pills, but most of them congregated to the side, talking amongst themselves and watching the lines.

"Oh, my God, I was so scared," I heard one woman say, a touch too loudly.

"No kidding," said a man at her elbow. "An emergency proving. I kept thinking, 'What if it's me? What if I was put in a thrall and ordered to forget it so that I didn't even know that I was?'"

"I checked my pockets," another man said. "I always do. Just in case I've got a poison pill in there or something that I'm supposed to use if I got caught."

"And what would you do if you found it?" the woman asked.

"Throw it as far away as I could!" the man said.

"It never works like that," the first man said dismissively.

They sounded so casual about it all. It made the possibilities they raised seem even more macabre.

Why had I said I wanted to see this? The scene was unpleasant—grotesque. I should have gone to my room, gotten cleaned up, gone to sleep and let this little drama play out however it would. It had nothing to do with me, I told myself. I didn't have to know about it.

Except that it had everything to do with me. One of these people's subversion might have almost killed me—and this bizarre scene was a fundamental part of how this strange world of Dorian's worked.

The world that had become mine.

A small commotion at the proving table attracted my attention. I recognized the woman at its center—she'd been the one in the gray dress who had been at my bedside when I woke. She'd kept her arm at her side when she stepped up to the table, looking like she was ready to flee.

"Hand," the agnate in front of her ordered, frowning at her.

The woman swayed, but she did not budge.

"Hand," the agnate repeated again.

Dorian finished with the person in front of him and motioned to forestall the next man from coming forward. He circled the table so that he stood behind the woman.

All around, the ballroom went silent, the conversations among those who had already been proven trailing off into silence as all eyes turned to the reluctant woman. The tension was so thick I could taste it.

"Put out your hand," Dorian said softly.

The command crackled across the room, the strength of it so great that I balled my hand into a fist even though I was not the one being addressed. The other humans in the room shifted as well, their hands twitching.

And still she did not obey.

"Now," the female agnate said.

What happened next was almost too fast to see. A lancet flashed, and Dorian held the woman, pinned and

45

screaming, as another agnate deftly prepared the pill. She tried to clench her teeth shut, but the female agnate pulled her jaw open as the pill was popped inside.

She continued to fight for two seconds, and then she went limp and began to sob.

"I'm sorry, Mr. Thorne!" she wailed. "I'm so sorry!"

CHAPTER SIX

Dorian glanced at the other three vampires. "You will screen the rest?"

The one who had prepared the last pill nodded. "Of course."

Dorian wrapped an arm around the woman, who was now clinging to his shirt as she sobbed, and guided her carefully to the edge of the room where I stood.

I felt a twinge—an instinctive jealousy of her proximity to him.

God, was I a piece of work.

"Oh, madam," she blubbered as she saw me, the words almost incomprehensible with her distress. "I swear I didn't mean to do it. I didn't want to do it!"

Dorian's expression was bleak. He spoke to me over her head. "Come to the study, Cora. You must decide what to do with her."

Me? Seriously?

I looked at the woman, who was clearly scared out of her mind. What to do with her. In her mind, I was certain that death was a very real possibility.

"Why?" I didn't want to have anything to do with this anymore. I wanted to go home, pull the covers over my head, and pretend everything was a dream.

But she was a real, live woman there, in front of me. Whatever else happened, I couldn't let her die for what some agnate had done to her.

I couldn't let Dorian kill her.

"Because you're the one she almost murdered." His answer was flat as he shepherded the hysterical woman up the stairs.

Unwillingly, I followed. From the salon, Dorian led the way to a room under the colonnade that I'd never seen before, opening the door and flipping on the lights to reveal a room with a club chair on either side of a long, low sofa. Books and curiosities crowded the shelves along the walls.

Dorian guided the woman to a chair and ordered her to sit.

She did. What else could she do?

He nodded to the chair opposite her, and I sat in it gingerly, wondering what, exactly, my role was supposed to be.

Dorian turned in front of the fireplace to face both of us.

"That's enough tears, Worth," he ordered.

I shivered at the authority in his voice. He wasn't allowing her the indulgence of crying. He had the power to deny it.

The woman nodded, and with a hiccough, she brushed the last tears away with her fingertips.

"When did it happen?" Dorian's voice was as impassive as his hooded eyes.

The woman took a deep, shuddering breath. "It was Christmas Eve, sir. I needed one more present—I'd forgotten to pick up the newest *Grand Theft Auto* for my brother—so I stopped by the Target near my house. She was waiting for me in the parking lot when I came out. I tried to fight her, but she was too strong."

"Did you see who it was?" he demanded.

"A djinn. She pulled me into the back of a van, and then she cut my arm up high, where no one would notice. She had the other blood ready, and she forced me to drink it. I'm so sorry!" Worth looked on the verge of bursting into tears again. "I never saw the agnate's face. I just heard his voice."

"It's a good thing you didn't see him," Dorian said. "If you had, he would have made sure that you wouldn't survive the proving, one way or another."

Worth nodded, relief spreading over her face.

Was I so obviously desperate for Dorian's approval? Was the queasiness in my stomach caused by the reflection of myself I saw in her face?

No, that wasn't me. I wouldn't let it be. No matter what he made me give him, I wouldn't let that be me.

"What did he ask?" Dorian prompted.

"He wanted to know about Cora Shaw—about the new mistress. He knew I was meant to be your cognate's lady's maid. That's why he grabbed me, because he knew I'd know whether she'd survived the conversion and become your new cognate."

"He already knew her name?" he asked sharply.

Worth trembled. "Yes. But he didn't know much about her because he asked me what she looked like and where she was right now. I told him she'd gone home."

"The conversion was five days before, at that point. I wonder what alerted him to her existence just then," Dorian mused, his eyes flickering over me. "If he had subverted you earlier, he might have gotten you to poison her IV line, avoiding the mess with the djinn he hired to come after her."

Christmas Eve. What was so special about Christmas Eve? A horrible realization was forming in my mind.

The woman looked even more stricken, if possible. "You shouldn't trust me anymore, sir. I can't hardly live with myself."

Dorian's mouth curved ever so slightly in an ironic echo of a smile. "I know, Worth. Believe me, I know. Yet you reacted no differently than anyone else would have."

He tilted his head as he looked at me, his face perfectly expressionless. "What do you want to do about her?"

"What do you mean?" I asked carefully. I felt that there might be a minefield in that question, if only I could see it.

"She is your lady's maid, but what she told that agnate nearly caused your death. Can you still trust her? Or do you believe that she should be dismissed? Or punished?" He asked the questions lightly, but his gaze on me was intense, searching.

The woman gave a tiny, dismayed cry. "I don't deserve to live, sir! Not after what I did."

I recoiled from them both. I couldn't even talk to her, not when she was like that. "She couldn't help it, could she?"

"Once she was subverted, she was in thrall to the agnate and could not refuse his orders, even when he wasn't present."

I didn't know what he was playing at. When he had spoken to Worth, every word had shivered with control. Now, his words were hollow, giving no hint of what he wanted me to say. I didn't want him to order me—the very idea made me sick—but I couldn't understand what the difference was in his mind, why he would choose to shape her reactions so cavalierly and to leave me guessing as to his intentions.

Whatever they were, her death was absolutely off the table.

"She's not…in thrall to him now, is she?" I asked carefully. "Or at any greater risk of being put back under his thrall?"

"No, when my blood is mixed with hers, the proving process returns her loyalty to me."

It was a test. But I didn't know what kind. If I failed to give the answer he desired, what would he do to me?

I looked at the woman across from me, her hands knotted anxiously in her lap. She didn't look all that much older than I was. It didn't seem right to talk over her head like she wasn't sitting right there, but she didn't seem able to protest.

It didn't matter what Dorian wanted me to say. Worth wasn't at fault for anything that had happened. In fact, I was beginning to suspect that I'd caused her to be snatched from the parking lot, however inadvertently. I wasn't going to let her take the blame at any level.

"I don't see that there is anything to be done," I said firmly. "What happened isn't her fault, and now she's as trustworthy as she ever was."

"Does that mean I will still be your lady's maid, madam?" The woman looked like she didn't even dare to fully believe it.

I shot Dorian a look. "If that's what you want— what you *really* want, not just what Dorian wants out of you—of course you can."

"Of course it's what I want, madam." There was a hint of outrage in her voice. "I applied for the scholarship when I was sixteen. I was one of six selected to complete years of study in fashion, cosmetology, interior decoration, administration and secretarial work, and event planning, and I beat out all the other candidates to win the position."

I rocked back slightly in the chair at that revelation. At the time that she had applied, there had been no cognate for her to serve—in fact, there was every possibility that Dorian would not have found a cognate during her lifetime. All that preparation for something that might never take place.

"If that's really how you feel, then I would be honored if you'd stay," I said weakly.

"Thank you, madam," Worth said fervently.

I winced and decided it wouldn't be too selfish for me to leverage the moment to get my way on one small thing.

"On one condition," I added.

The woman looked nervous again. "Yes, madam?"

"That you stop calling me 'madam' and call me 'Cora' instead," I said.

Worth looked scandalized. She opened her mouth, then closed it. After several long seconds while the conflict played out on her face, she nodded. "If that is your wish...Cora."

"It absolutely is."

Dorian shifted in front of the fireplace, and I turned to him instantly—and felt a small disquiet as I realized that Worth had done the same thing, with as much attention reflected in her body as I felt in mine.

"Cora's judgment will stand," he said. "You must not feel guilty. You weren't responsible for your actions. I was. I should have protected you, too."

Worth sagged, as if a sentence had just been lifted from her. Dorian wasn't just reassuring her. He was ordering her—telling her what to think, what to feel. I could feel his influence in every word.

"Thank you, sir," she murmured.

"You may go now, until tomorrow. And have a good night."

"Good night, sir." Still sniffing slightly, the woman rose from the chair, gave a deep nod of her head, and left.

Dorian stood silently for a long moment, looking at

me.

I stared back, trying to read his emotions in the impassive lines of his face. What exactly was that all about?

"You approve," I said finally. "You were judging me. Seeing what I would do. What would you have done if I had said that I wanted her to be punished?"

Dorian's wave was dismissive. "I was certain that you wouldn't."

I narrowed my eyes at him. "No, you weren't. You might have been pretty sure, but you wouldn't have asked if you were really certain."

He moved over to the chair that Worth had left and sprawled in it in a single graceful, loose-limbed motion. His posture was casual, but I could feel the undercurrents growing between us again, now that we were alone, and I knew he was deliberately putting distance between us.

And I was acutely aware that I was wearing absolutely nothing under the coat he had given me. I shifted uncomfortably. The corner of his mouth twitched at the movement, but he said nothing about it.

"You are as much a stranger to me as I am to you, Cora. It takes time for us to get to know each other."

"The appropriate time to get to know someone is before you drink their blood and bond them to you forever," I said.

Also before you screw them senseless in a coat closet, a part of my brain pointed out helpfully.

Yeah. That, too.

"Perhaps," he mused. "Perhaps one day, we will

have that luxury."

I knew he wasn't talking specifically about me but about all of his kind. I closed my eyes, shivering slightly with the horror of everything that had happened that day. I wished that I could believe that I was safer now than I had been when I was running from the djinn.

But I couldn't be sure. Dorian could control me as easily as Worth had been controlled by the other agnate—more, even.

How did I know that I wouldn't become a puppet for Dorian? What person could not give in to the temptation to make his lover in the image of his fantasy, if he had the power?

I wasn't sure that I could have that level of self-restraint.

"You changed her," I said aloud, opening my eyes again. "Worth. You…rummaged around in her head and changed things around. You told her not to blame herself, and so she didn't. She couldn't."

Dorian's eyes were hard, like chipped sapphires. "She had a compulsion to protect my privacy, to betray no information about her employment here that might compromise me. That is what I require of every human in my service. Yet she betrayed me, however unwillingly, and she knew it. If I had left her with both the impulse and the guilt, it very well could have driven her to her death. Is that better to you?"

I shuddered. "Of course not."

I wanted to protest against using any kind of compulsion at all. But it was becoming clear to me that such a position just wasn't possible for a vampire. He had too many enemies in other vampires, and if unaffected humans were ever allowed to find out who lived among them, they would try to stamp them all out.

Could I blame them? If he hadn't gotten into my head, wouldn't I want his kind destroyed, too?

"You could do that to me, too," I said. "Demand complete loyalty. Complete submission. A bond—that would be even stronger than a thrall."

"Yes. But I needn't do anything so drastic. A bond can stand on its own. I have no reason to…tamper to that extent."

To that extent. That meant that he would change more than the bond already had if he did see the reason. What would that require? If I'd given the wrong answer, told him I wanted Worth to die—would that have offended him to the extent that he would choose to rewrite that part of me?

I looked at the beautiful creature across from me, a physical approximation of a man—no, an improvement upon one. No real man was that perfect, no man could make my blood sing in my veins, make my heart beat in terror and desire.

I couldn't imagine him without all that, tangled together, the darkness and the terrible light.

I shook myself—shook my head to try to clear it of the fog that was beginning to trickle in again. I seized on what I'd meant to ask him as soon as Worth had left the room.

"Has Dr. Robeson sent you many…candidates in the past?"

Dorian raised an eyebrow at my sudden change of

subject. "Yes, of course. Cancer patients are ideal for our cause because they receive a terminal diagnosis weeks, if not months, before they die."

"Well, she also knew that I'd decided to—to try the procedure with you. So she knew I was going in. And then on Christmas Eve, I scheduled a new appointment with her through the online patient portal. So she would have known that I either changed my mind—or I survived. Do you think she…?" I trailed off. I had no idea what Dr. Robeson or anyone else might or might not do. Not in the thrall of a vampire.

I said, "I made an appointment at the university Health Center, too, for eleven tomorrow morning, but the appointment with Dr. Robeson seems more likely to be the leak, considering."

Dorian's jaw clenched briefly, then released. "If my enemies found out about Dr. Robeson's role in identifying candidates, subverting her would have been a poor choice. I would have found out what had happened at her next proving, so they could only try it once and for a short period of time."

"Then how?"

"It may have been someone else who has access to her medical records and her schedule—nurses, other doctors in her practice, something of that sort. She may have made coded notes when one of her terminal patients decided to accept my offer, or maybe she mentioned you in some way to a coworker that tipped him off. You would have triggered his attention by scheduling another appointment when you should have been dead."

"A spy network in the hospital." It had been strange enough to think that one vampire had agents working for him at Johns Hopkins. The idea that there were others who were tracking them was even more disturbing.

He nodded curtly. "I will have my men look into it. Good thinking, Cora."

Good thinking. He said it in the same tone that a human might tell a dog 'good girl' when it had done something unexpectedly clever.

Could he read my mind? Sometimes I wasn't sure, but he certainly didn't seem to notice that thought. He stood and closed the distance between us to stand in front of the chair I was sitting in.

He bent, and I tilted my face up to his—so eager, so hungry for his touch. He cupped my cheek in one hand and kissed me slowly, thoroughly. I gave myself up to it even as I remembered the impatience of his mouth before, the hardness of it, the feel of his teeth on my neck....

He pulled back.

"Goodnight, Cora. Get a shower. I'm needed in Baltimore tonight."

And with that, he was gone.

CHAPTER SEVEN

I reached for my phone reflexively when I woke the next morning. My hand struck empty wood, and I peeled my slitted eyes the rest of the way open and blinked several times, trying to process the canopy bed, wide windows, and heavy smell of flowers.

Oh, yeah. I'd spent the night in the vampire's house. Because that was such a good idea.

Except that it really was the safest place for me right now. Which was the most frightening thought of all.

"Good morning, Cora."

I nearly jumped out of my skin at the voice. I whipped my head around to see Worth sitting in a chair against the wall. She set aside the tablet she had been using.

I muttered a curse under my breath as my heart rate slowly returned to normal.

I pushed up in bed. I hadn't been able to figure out how to work the shower the night before. There'd been at least half a dozen knobs and an honest-to-goodness touch-screen interface. So instead, I'd taken a very long bath to soak the blood out of my hair and the knots out of my muscles, and then I'd found a silky little camisole and shorts set in one of the drawers in the closet, choosing the least frilly pair of undies I could find to go underneath. T-shirts were more my usual style, but all the ones in the closet had designer labels that made me feel guilty about sleeping in them.

I rubbed the sleep out of my eyes.

"For future reference, I'd rather not have you sitting in the room while I'm sleeping," I said, sounding crankier than I intended. But dammit, her watching me sleep was creepy. "If I need you, I'll call."

"Yes, m—Cora," the woman said. She sat primly, acting as if the events of the night before had never happened. "Mr. Thorne told me that you'd say that. He also told me that you wouldn't call, so he asked me to sit in. There's a button that rings the bell next to the bed," she added helpfully. "We also have a house app, if you'd like to install that on your phone."

"No, thanks," I said. "I lost my phone, anyway."

"Oh, I have it," she said, reaching into her pocket. She pulled out a phone—my actual phone, in its Hello Kitty case I'd grabbed from a bargain bin. "It was found where you dropped it."

I slid out of bed and took it from her before she could do more than stand up. Hello Kitty's dot-eyed face was a little scuffed, but the screen wasn't even scratched. I pushed the button to wake it up, and the lock screen lit up with the picture that I'd gotten the bartender to take of everybody at Hannah's twenty-first birthday bash.

Just looking at it made my heart do a little flip-flop in my chest. I tightened my hand around it.

"Thanks," I said.

It has tracking software on it, I thought as I checked for new messages. Dorian had hacked it somehow— he'd said as much.

As unsettling as it was to think about, I couldn't fault him for it now. Not after what had happened.

"And as for calling you—I'll use the bell," I said. "Promise. Just as long as you don't hang out in my room while I'm sleeping."

I looked around the room for telltale cameras, re-membering the bank of video monitors in the room off the foyer. I'd been too tired the night before to think or care about it. But I did both now. "No video, either. Not cool."

"I'll let Mr. Thorne know," Worth murmured.

"Okay," I said, not sure if that would actually change anything.

Yeah, probably not.

I stepped past Worth and into the bathroom, clos-ing the door with a firm, "Excuse me," when she tried to follow.

The silk fabric of the shorts whispered over my

legs—the night before, I had shaved for the first time in over a week. It felt almost scandalously decadent to feel clean and smooth and strong again.

To feel healthy.

Thanks to Dorian.

I regarded my refection as I brushed my teeth, color in my cheeks that hadn't been there in months. Where had Dorian gone, the night before? What kind of business did he have in Baltimore?

I wondered if he would tell me if I asked. I wondered if I wanted to know.

I wondered where he was now because I missed him.

With quick, irritated strokes, I brushed out my hair. Withdrawal, I decided. I was having withdrawal symptoms. I wondered—with time and distance, could they go away?

Hi, I'm Cora and I'm a vampire addict, I thought.

Hi, Cora.

I made a face at my reflection and emerged from the bathroom to find Worth waiting patiently for me again. I should be able to talk to her—another human, another woman in the vampire's mansion.

Except that I wasn't human. Not anymore. And she might be a human, but she was in his thrall.

"I have appointments today," I said to her instead of all the other thoughts that crowded in my head. "Two of them."

I wasn't sure if it was really safe to go. Dorian had said I wouldn't be in any more danger directly once the puppets that had been set in motion had been dealt with, but I wasn't sure I wanted to gamble my life on that.

On the other hand, I couldn't spend the rest of my life hidden away in Dorian's mansion.

Could I?

"Mr. Thorne left a message," Worth said. "He said he'll accompany you today."

"He could just email," I pointed out. "Or text, like everyone else. He doesn't have to play a kid's game of telephone."

"I'll let him know," Worth said.

By carrying my own message back to him. Right. Was that a glimmer of humor I saw in her eyes?

And as for Dorian coming with me…. Yeah, that was going to be awkward. My first appointment was at the Health Center to get a birth control prescription. I didn't feel like telling him that I didn't trust his word that I couldn't get pregnant. But I also wanted the pills.

Hell, I still didn't know where baby vampires came from. And that seemed like a pretty important point, given that we'd had sex twice in as many days.

When I'd made my second appointment, I'd wanted to see Dr. Robeson because I'd thought she was an impartial authority who could verify whether I really was cured. Now I knew she was just another one of Dorian's…minions, thralls, whatever, I wasn't sure if there was a point.

I didn't plan on explaining that to Dorian, either.

There was a knock at the door.

"That will be breakfast," Worth said, going to open it. "I ordered it when you started to stir."

"Thanks," I said weakly as she took an overloaded tray from a woman outside. My appetite had come back with a vengeance over the past couple of days, but that was enough food for at least four people. "You should tell the chef that I'm really flattered. And impressed."

"Oh, you will have to tell him that yourself, Cora," Worth said, setting the tray onto a small round table. "As soon as you've finished, I'll help you dress, and I'll message Mr. Thorne that you're ready to go."

"Help me...?" She might as well have offered to brush my teeth for me.

"Of course, Cora," she agreed brightly, pulling out the chair and smiling hopefully at me until I sat.

Of course.

CHAPTER EIGHT

When I came downstairs, Dorian was waiting for me by the front door, the collar of his clean-lined pea coat turned up around his face and a pair of aviators dangling from one hand. My chest squeezed at the sight of him, and I had to stop myself from running down the last flight of stairs.

Not away from him, this time, but into his arms.

He caught me with a hand on my shoulder, holding me at a distance even as his keen regard communicated with perfect clarity all the things he would like to be doing to me instead. I swayed slightly in his grasp, echoes of the lust and terror of the night before coming over me again.

"That is quite enough of the U.S.T., you two."

I tore my gaze from Dorian and noticed his companion for the first time, a slender female with lips the color of fresh blood.

Another vampire. After my time with Dorian, it was impossible to mistake her for an ordinary woman. She had his unnatural perfection, but more than that was the sense of power that surrounded her, as if she were larger than her physical body.

"Clarissa Kerr, allow me to present Cora Shaw," Dorian said.

"Charmed, I sure," she purred, holding out her hand, each nail shining with red lacquer.

I was dressed in designer clothes from the closet Worth had stocked—well, all except for my running shoes—because nothing else of what I'd worn the night before was in a fit state to wear. I'd always admired Lisette's fashion sense, but Worth was a clothing genius, able to put together an outfit at a glance that looked better on me than any clothes had a right to look. Even so, next to Clarissa, I felt downright frumpy.

She burst into laughter when I took her hand gingerly, and she shook with a businesslike firmness.

"Don't worry, girl, I'm not going to eat you!" she said. "I'm one of the good guys."

Dorian cast her a quelling look. "You will have to excuse Clarissa. She is very young and enjoys a certain amount of mischief."

She laughed again. "He's lucky I do, or else I might not find it so entertaining to be an Adelphoi. The subversiveness of the young, and all that."

I smiled somewhat tightly, not sure what she meant. Next to her, I knew I looked like a homely, ungainly adolescent. The easy camaraderie between her and Dorian left me feeling very much like the odd one out.

"Put your hackles down," the woman advised, sliding sunglasses up her nose until her raised eyebrows arched perfectly over the edge. "I don't want him—and he certainly doesn't want me. Or has he not explained that to you yet?"

"Clarissa," Dorian said warningly.

She pouted, flipping a gauzy veil over her thick auburn hair. "I don't have a cognate, Dorian. Why don't you let me play with yours?"

He ignored her. "Clarissa and I are going to come with you today to make sure you stay safe."

"My last bodyguards didn't help," I pointed out.

A brief shadow of a smile flickered across his face. "They weren't agnates."

"You said that a djinn is stronger than a vampire," I countered.

"But now there are two, and we're armed. And the political fallout of attacking an agnate, directly or otherwise, is quite a bit different from killing a few humans and a cognate who does not yet officially exist."

He let go of me to put his sunglasses on, and I mirrored the motion. The butler opened the door, and we stepped into the blinding light.

Privately, I wondered how much defense the slender Clarissa could manage, vampire or not. But as she twitched her coat, I caught a glimpse of the bulky butt of a gun and the hilts of a nasty-looking assortment of bladed weapons.

Perhaps she was entitled to a little more benefit of the doubt.

One of the Escalades waited at the curb for us. I examined the passenger side window for evidence of damage as the driver held the back door open for us, but there was no mark on the glass. Either it was different SUV than the one I'd been in the night before, or it had already been repaired.

"The UMD Health Center," Dorian told the driver.

"Yes, sir."

Clarissa ducked in first. She even scooted across the bench seat gracefully. I followed, taking the center seat.

My skin prickled to be so close to her. Unlike Dorian, her persuasion had no effect on me, so I could clearly hear the little primal voice in the back of my head sounding the alarm.

She was a predator. She ate people like me. Perhaps she preferred men—I had no idea—but any human would probably do in a pinch.

Only two things kept me from bolting: Dorian's presence and his revelation the night before that if she did bite me, it would kill her as surely as it did me.

I relaxed infinitesimally as Dorian settled in beside me and shut the door, pressing as close to him as I dared without drawing attention to my movement. He glanced down, the smallest frown creasing his forehead.

Whatever he saw in my face made him hook his arm around my shoulders and pull my head so that it rested against his strong chest. I could feel the bulk of the pistol at his side, but I still I sank into him gratefully, accepting the reaction his touch called from me as the car rolled away. At the same time, I marveled at how far into the insanity I'd fallen to find anything comforting about his closeness.

"This is a great victory for us, Cora," he said. "It will all be worth it in the end."

To who? I didn't ask the question aloud. I'm not entirely sure he would have understood.

I tilted my head up to meet his eyes. "Why are you taking me to my appointments?"

"You want to go, and it should be safe."

"Yes, but you're worried enough about it that you've called a friend for protection. Why not tell me to reschedule? Or just say no?"

"I believe that it's very important that I do not."

I saw a flash deep in his eyes and with it came comprehension. If he refused, he had to either restrain me or convince me. And with either choice, he didn't fully trust himself not to use his powers over me.

The only thing I didn't understand was why he cared. He clearly had no problem at all rummaging in Worth's head. Was I different because I was a cognate?

Was it because he cared about me? Or was that, too, some obscure political point—or perhaps, even more sinisterly, that it would represent the first step on the road to losing control?

Whatever the reason he restrained himself now, I had no doubt that he would use all his power if the stakes were high enough.

Dorian broke the silence. "The staff at the oncology unit has been proven and the leak was found. It was one of the receptionists."

Proven. That meant that every one of the staff members who had not been in Dorian's thrall now was. I shuddered a little, wondering just how many people in the world were walking around with a little bit of vampire in their brains and didn't even know it.

Dorian didn't seem to notice my reaction as he continued. "The unit should be secure now, at least for a short while. Even so, our enemies must already know about your appointment, and though you should be safe now, it seems excessively foolhardy right now to show up at a place and time where you're expected."

"So you're canceling the appointment?" I asked. He'd just said that he wasn't....

"Relocating, merely," Dorian said. "My staff found a nearby doctor's office where you could meet Dr. Robeson, and LabCorp can handle any tests that she orders."

I wondered if Dorian guessed the reason I wanted my appointments. I wondered what he'd think if he did.

I'd prepared a cover story for the presence of my unusual companions at the university Health Center, but it ended up being unnecessary. The receptionist's eyes seemed to slide right past them, as did the nurse's when she brought me in to take my weight—I'd cracked triple-digits again, I discovered with delight—temperature, and blood pressure.

Typically, they sent me off for a urine-based pregnancy test, too. It was a running joke that the Health Center diagnosed everything from mono to a skinned knee as pregnancy unless you took a test to prove otherwise.

Except for my short stop in the restroom, Dorian kept close and Clarissa only a little farther away as she repeatedly consulted the screen of a small device she held in her hand. When the nurse showed me to the examination room, I stopped in the doorway before either of the agnates could follow.

There was no way I was going to ask the doctor for birth control pills with Dorian looming and Clarissa laughing at me.

"You can wait outside," I said with all the authority I could put into my voice.

Seeing Dorian's hesitation, I added, "Look, you can see that the room is empty. There's only one door. And the doctor will be along in just a few minutes."

Dorian and Clarissa exchanged coded looks, as if there was something that I didn't know that they weren't ready to tell me yet. After a moment, Clarissa seemed to surrender, giving a small shrug.

"Your cognate," she said, and she waved the screen of her device before taking station just outside the door.

Dorian gave a tight nod. "I will be just outside. If you need anything at all—*call for me.*"

I swallowed and nodded back, stepping all the way into the room and shutting the door. I hoped I wasn't being reckless, but I couldn't make decisions based on what I didn't know.

The doctor—or nurse practitioner, as it turned out—asked a few questions about my sexual activity and health history and wrote a birth control prescription. Flanked by my two guards, I filled it at the pharmacy, and before Dorian could read the label, I shoved the paper bag into the Kate Spade purse I was carrying, which looked like a rather attractive chartreuse doily.

Dorian showed no interest in the appointment or my prescription. I'd thought he would say something, do something. After all his talk about how I belonged to him, forever, I'd thought that getting between me and my doctors would be a matter of course.

He didn't seem to care. And that made me feel both petty, for thinking that it would matter to him, and disturbed, because it was obvious that Dorian was preoccupied, and whatever it was that made my trip seem trivial couldn't be good news for me.

For her part, Clarissa, if anything, appeared amused by the entire excursion, but it was amusement with a cutting edge, an air of barely contained violence that made me shy away any time her judging gaze slid across me. I had the sense that she regarded me like a particularly valuable puppy that needed to be taken out for a walk, if there were a slight possibility that such a walk could end in a bloodbath.

The SUV picked us up at the curb in front of the Health Clinic. A delicious smell hit me when the driver opened the door, and I discovered that he'd gone by an Italian restaurant for carryout during my appointment.

"Help yourself," Dorian said as the SUV pulled away.

I looked inside and frowned. There was only one entrée inside.

"What about you?" I asked, looking at them in turn.

Clarissa chuckled. "She really *is* new, isn't she? We're not hungry. We only need one meal a day—though we often eat two, if only for the amusement of it."

"Right," I said, flushing. Dorian had already explained that he needed less food than a human. I'd just forgotten about it.

But my embarrassment and the reminder of their alien nature, however disquieting, couldn't affect my appetite. I dug in, the lasagna quickly disappeared, and I packed my trash back into the bag and put it between my feet. Having meals appear on cue was a perk I felt like I could get used to.

Neither of the vampires seemed interested in small talk—and with perfect honesty, I admitted to myself that the less that Clarissa said, the happier I was.

Squeezed between the agnates, I pulled out my phone, its familiar weight reassuring in my hand. Reflexively, I went into my messages. Hannah, Ross, Sarah, and Geoff had all left me texts since finals, along with the flood of generic "Merry Christmas!" wishes from half the people in my contact list.

With a pang of guilt, I realized I hadn't even had a chance to read them since I woke up in Dorian Thorne's house two days before. I busied myself with replying to my friends, tapping out banal comments and adding reassurances that I was doing much better to those who knew about my cancer.

It felt strange, like I was writing as myself from an alternate life.

Glancing up at the rearview mirror as we took the

exit off the Baltimore-Washington Parkway, I realized that the Escalade wasn't alone. At least two other vehicles had been behind us since we left College Park—and any doubt I had that we were being followed was dispelled when they made the second turn behind us.

"Do you know about those other cars?" I asked Dorian. "The blue sedan and the gray minivan?"

Dorian flashed a brief shadow of a smile. "They're ours," he said.

"Good work, those men. Very subtle. Let's hope the Kyrioi don't have the observational skills of a twenty-year-old cognate," Clarissa grumbled.

Dorian simply shrugged as the SUV stopped in front of an unfamiliar medical center. The driver opened the door, and I scrambled out after Dorian.

"Did these doctors send you patients, too?" I asked, looking up at the building.

Dorian fell into step beside me as I walked the short distance to the clinic door. "They still do. I'm not the only agnate who is participating in my research, Cora."

"Oh," I said, feeling suddenly stupid. Of course there were others. Otherwise, what was the point? I hadn't thought about that possibility. I'd been far too wrapped up in my own personal drama.

"But we could always count on him to keep all the best ones for himself," Clarissa said cheerfully behind us.

"We were hardly in competition," Dorian returned. "And I don't recall you complaining about any of the men you were sent."

Men who were now dead. I hugged myself as Dorian held the door open for me to enter. I stepped past him into the waiting room.

Men who would have been dead anyway, I reminded myself. Dorian only offered his test to people with terminal illnesses and a very short time to live. And I knew from my own experience that he told them the odds and gave them a choice—and even insisted that they make the choice two weeks after their screening came back positive so that they had a chance to think rationally about their decision, away from all agnatic influence.

Just as he had with me.

And if they took his offer, it was because, like me, they thought the gamble was worth it.

They'd been wrong. I'd been right. That was the only difference between us. Still, Clarissa's offhand reference to causing the deaths of who-knows-how-many people chilled me.

I signed in at the desk and was soon called back, repeating the weight, blood pressure, temperature routine before being shown to an exam room. This time, Dorian made no move to follow me, even though he seemed even more tense than before.

"Tell me if I'm being stupid, Dorian," I said in the doorway. "My life's not worth keeping you out of this room."

He blinked at me as if I'd taken him off guard—*What, you don't expect common sense from a cognate?*—and cast a glance at Clarissa. She consulted the device and shrugged.

"It looks clear."

His shoulders eased slightly. "You will be fine, Cora. It's paranoia, nothing more."

I looked from one to the other. "Okay, then," I said.

Almost as soon as the door was shut, Dr. Robeson rapped and came in. Not having to wait was apparently another prerogative of Dorian's cognate.

Dr. Robeson's expression was avid as she entered and pulled her stethoscope from around her neck.

"I'm so happy to see you, Cora. You survived," she said. "You were cured."

"The first," I agreed stiffly.

I didn't know what to say to her anymore. I'd trusted her—trusted her with my treatment, trusted her with my life. Her referral to Dorian had saved me, but it still felt like a betrayal. She was his creature, contaminated by his control, not the impartial medical expert I had counted upon.

"This really is…remarkable." She stretched the collar of my shirt to put the cold end of the stethoscope against my chest, then spent a minute pressing it against various points of my back to listen to my lungs. She took my wrist in her hand, holding her fingers against it to take my pulse even though it had already been registered with my blood pressure.

She started to drop my hand, then spied the scarlet tear-drop on the inside on my wrist and turned it so that she could examine it more carefully in the light.

"Remarkable," she repeated. "Do you know what this is?"

"Yes," I said, pulling my arm away. "You understand it? Really understand it? You know what *he* is?"

"And what you are now. It must be a terrific shock. But you must also be aware of the many benefits—"

I cut her off. "Yes. I am. But I didn't choose this. Not really. It chose me."

"You didn't choose cancer, either. Of all the unwanted things in the world, you could do far worse," she pointed out.

"I really am cured, then?" I asked. I knew I was, but I didn't trust my own mind anymore. Not when Dorian's mere presence could make me believe anything at all.

"There are only two outcomes, Cora, cured or dead." Dr. Robeson took my hand again and pushed up my sleeve. Before I could react, she palmed something from the tray on the rolling table next to her and made a quick flicking motion along my lower arm.

I yelped in pain as the blood welled up from the nick she'd just made. She set the scalpel back on the tray and swiftly took up a small gauze pad, wiping it across my skin.

The cut was already sealed, only a pale line revealing that there had ever been a wound.

"What the hell," I snarled, yanking my arm back as she released me.

"That is the most definitive test I know," she said calmly. "If you want your lymphocytes to be checked, I can do that, but we both already know the answer."

"I do want them checked," I said stubbornly.

"Very well, then." She dug in the top drawer and came up with a blood collection kit.

I straightened my arm at her order, and she pulled the rubberized tourniquet strap tight around it.

"What do I do now?" I said. "I just wanted my old life back. Not this."

I didn't want to confide in Dr. Robeson—I didn't trust her, not anymore—but I had to talk to someone who wouldn't think I was crazy, and she was a better candidate than someone like Worth who worked every day under Dorian's roof.

She slipped the needle into my vein and popped the collection bottle into place as she pulled the tourniquet loose with the other hand.

"You do what every cancer survivor does who has lost something precious to them. You mourn what's gone. And you embrace your new future." She looked suddenly old, and I knew that she was thinking that my future would be much longer than hers.

Yeah. If no one killed me first.

Putting the collection tube aside and pulling out the needle, she continued, "I've been in oncology for a long time, and there are hundreds of patients in Johns Hopkins right now who would give up a great deal more than what you have to gain another year, even another month. They've lost breasts, limbs, organs—even had pieces of their brains cut out—just for the chance at a cure. And what have you lost, really?"

I thought of everything Dorian Thorne offered me—agelessness, health, wealth, and not least of all, himself. Who wouldn't want that?

No one, of course. The answer was simple. No one would turn that offer down—because no one could.

What I'd lost couldn't be measured, like a hand or an eye. I'd lost my freedom. Myself. I'd given it away, and I'd keep giving it away until I died. Which might be much sooner than Dr. Robeson believed.

"I'll send this out for the tests," Dr. Robeson said. "You can check your results online, as usual."

With a sick feeling in my stomach, I recognized a slight light of envy in her eyes as she looked me over. She wished she was in my place. Knowing the devil's bargain I'd taken, she still wished that she had the bond.

She patted my shoulder before stopping at the door. "Congratulations, Cora. Even without the test, I can tell you right now that you have nothing to be concerned about."

Nothing, I thought. Nothing at all.

CHAPTER NINE

"I'd like to get some stuff from my apartment," I said as the SUV rolled away from the curb. "If it's safe, I mean."

The clothes Worth had picked out for me were far more stylish and flattering than anything I owned, but they weren't mine. I wanted my own comb, my own toothbrush. My own shampoo.

Dorian and Clarissa exchanged another look. I was beyond sick of it.

"Look, why don't you two just tell me what the hell is going on?" I snapped. "Why do you think I might get attacked in empty rooms, and why is Clarissa staring at that whatever-it-is for?"

There was a ringing silence for a long moment, and

finally, Dorian said, "Djinn can be slippery. They fool human eyes more easily than agnatic senses, but a good measure of caution is always wise when we deal with them. Clarissa's tool helps us detect if there is one about, even if we don't see it."

"They're not normally social creatures—unlike agnates," Clarissa said, and I couldn't tell whether she was being sarcastic about the last bit. "But one of them could very well take offense at the, uh, neutralization of the other djinn last night. And when someone hires one assassin, there's good reason to believe that he might hire more."

"So is it safe for me to go to my apartment?" I asked. "Or not? Just tell me. I'm not going to pitch a fit if I can't get my way."

"It *should* be safe," Clarissa said. "It should be as safe as it ever is for any cognate, now."

"And how safe is that?" I pressed.

"Untouchable," she said simply. "No one should dare to harm a hair on your head. Follow you, yes. Spy on you? Absolutely, especially after Dorian's invitation yesterday. But if you should step out in front of a speeding truck, it's their duty to try to save you, even if they're Dorian's sworn enemies."

"So what's all this about, then?" I made a motion to include her and the other cars that were following discreetly behind.

"Paranoia," Dorian broke in. "But I would not have survived as long as I have without it."

"They shouldn't have attacked you the first time," Clarissa said to me. "But that was merely…bad form.

81

Not practically unheard of, like it is now."

"Bad form," I repeated. I didn't consider killing people to be bad form.

"Once you are properly introduced, I will pull the escort," Dorian said.

"Until then, you'll have a bigger entourage than Michael Jackson," Clarissa added brightly. "But he's dead, isn't he? Well, someone else famous, then."

"So my apartment?" I pressed.

"Should be fine," Clarissa said. "Really, Dorian, you think scaring her like this is worth it?"

I just looked at Dorian.

Finally, he nodded. "It should be fine."

"Okay, then," I said. "Let's get my things."

Dorian gave the order to the driver, and we drove to campus in silence.

As the Escalade approached the entrance to my apartment building, I spotted my Gramma's Ford Focus in the parking lot. I craned my neck around, looking for signs of damage, but it appeared to be in perfect repair. As if nothing had happened at all. And there was the SUV behind it in the almost-empty lot, its bumper in perfect condition even though I had slammed a djinn's body against it the day before.

"My people work quickly," Dorian said, catching the direction of my gaze.

"No kidding."

Clarissa was frowning at her screen. "Looks like we have company."

"Where?" Dorian's attention snapped to her instantly.

But Clarissa had already unbuckled, and her hand was on the door handle. "Oh, I've been waiting for the chance to play with my little toys! See you in a moment."

She flashed a bright, perfect smile as she slid the sunglasses over her eyes. Then, far faster than any human could move, she was gone out of the still-moving Escalade.

I watched out of the window as she sprinted toward the corner of the apartment building, closing the distance in the time that it took me to draw a breath. She pulled an ugly-looking object out of her belt as she ran, holding it in front of her like a weapon as she slapped something at her waist.

Suddenly, she seemed to flicker, as if she were only half there, her motions jerky like an old film movie played too slowly. There were spaces between her motions, and in one of those spaces, she swung around, the object held up at something I couldn't see. A sudden light shot from it, and a crackling kind of bang, and suddenly, she was clinging to a man with one arm wrapped around his neck and the other with the weapon pointed at his temple.

She gave a blood-curdling whoop, her face split in a grin.

Others came sprinting from across the parking lot, spilling out of the blue sedan and the gray minivan. More vampires, moving at inhuman speeds. A cord or rope appeared from somewhere, and one of the agnates quickly, roughly bound the man's hands.

Clarissa stepped away then, pulled out the screen

she'd been consulting earlier, and called, "That's it! All clear!"

Our SUV reached the curb, and Dorian didn't wait for the driver to circle around. He pushed the door open and landed on the sidewalk.

"Come, Cora," he ordered.

Right. A man had just appeared out of nowhere, and people had been trying to kill me just yesterday. Why wouldn't I want to come out?

Despite that thought, I didn't think Dorian was going to get me killed, so I unbuckled, hooked my purse over my shoulder, and scooted over. At the doorway, Dorian scooped me up unceremoniously—and ran.

The scream got caught in my throat, and I managed only a strangled kind of gasp. The pavement blurred under his feet only a few feet below my body. My hands spasmed around his shoulders in sheer terror at the speed that shouldn't have been possible outside of a car.

He stopped in front of the other agnates and set my feet gently on the ground. I had to order myself to unclench my hands to regain my own balance. Every time I thought I knew where I was with him or in his world, he did something that turned my brains inside out.

"Next time, a little warning, please," I managed.

Dorian didn't answer. I didn't even think he had noticed my reaction. All his attention was on the disheveled man in the center of the circle of agnates, who was reeling about and tugging ineffectually at the bonds that pinned his wrists. I had an instinctive pity for the paunchy man, ringed by the tall, powerful, beautiful predators. He seemed so absurd, so ordinary and pitiful.

Then his gaze slid past mine, and his eyes burned yellow, just for just an instant.

I recoiled so hard that I jerked back into Dorian's chest. The last creature I'd met with yellow eyes had tried to kill me.

Another djinn.

"Hey, hey, hey!" the djinn was shouting. "Easy, there! Easy!"

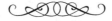

CHAPTER TEN

"I was just hired to watch, I swear," the djinn wailed. "Look in my pocket. Go ahead. Look!"

Disdainfully, Clarissa reached into the bulging pocket of his jacket—and came up with a compact camera body with a small zoom lens.

"See? I was watching, that's all!"

"What does your employer want?" Dorian demanded.

"Oh, the usual things," the djinn said. "What she looks like. When she comes, when she goes. Who her friends are. There's nothing wrong with that, right?"

The ring of agnates shifted slightly, but no one spoke.

The little man—the djinn—held up his bound hands imploringly. "Come on, Dalton. You've hired me before yourself. You can vouch for me."

One of the vampires, a tall man with silver-shot hair and crow's feet that looked like they were being worn for effect, nodded reluctantly.

"It's Finnegan Cage. I know him."

"Tell them what kind of work I do," he urged.

"Strictly shadow-work," Dalton said. "I've never heard a rumor otherwise."

"See? See?" Finnegan was getting so worked up that he was all but caroming from vampire to vampire. "No wet work here! Not me! Now get these damned salt-bonds off me so I can go about my business."

"Who hired you?" Dorian didn't look impressed.

"Oh, you know I can't tell you that," Finnegan said plaintively. "What kind of shadow would I be if I went around blabbing everyone's business?"

"You just blabbed Dalton's," Clarissa pointed out.

"Oh, no," Finnegan said. "You can't say that. That was a really long time ago. Decades. And I didn't tell you what it was, did I? And anyhow, I don't know. Some little wisp came up to me at The Plant, an intermediary, and I wasn't going to say no, was I? It was good work. Fair work. *Clean* work." He emphasized the last point.

Looking irritated, Dorian let out a puff of air. "Let the imp go."

Clarissa made a disappointed face, but she gave the cord a tug, and it fell from Finnegan's hands.

And then the man...*shifted*. Just a moment before,

he had looked small and unimportant and certainly unthreatening, a stark contrast to the agnates who encircled him. But now I could see that the thickness at his center wasn't fat but corded muscle, and his disarrayed hair had a dangerous edge instead of a foolish one. He grew wider, taller as he stepped back, the heavy lines of his face rearranging themselves into a more sinister mask.

Finnegan backed away slowly, still keeping an eye on the agnates. They were all on edge, I saw, shifting slightly in response to his movements.

As foolish as he'd just seemed, I realized that the djinn—little man no longer—would be a dangerous opponent if he chose.

"You and your damned tech toys," Finnegan spat. "You weren't always on top, you know. And you won't be forever. Put those away, and you'd never see me coming—until it was far too late."

Then he simply blinked out of existence.

Clarissa looked at her screen device for several seconds, and I saw others in the group pull their own out.

"All right, then," she said finally. "He's really gone."

"You really believe him?" Dorian asked Dalton.

Dalton shrugged. "I've known him for a very long time. He doesn't like to stir up trouble. I don't think he'd take anything but shadow-work. He never has done before that I know about."

"It's a good thing, Dorian," said Clarissa. "If there's shadow-work about, no one will want to get caught doing more. Too many eyes."

"I don't trust djinn," Dorian muttered, his hand tightening fractionally around my upper arm.

"That's because you're a xenophobe," Clarissa said succinctly. "Come on, now. If you're going to let your cognate get some things from her apartment—let her! She really is safe now."

Dorian nodded reluctantly. "Fine. Let's go."

"I'll be waiting in the car," Clarissa said.

Dorian hesitated. Behind the impassivity of his expression, I knew he was torn. Finally, he nodded.

"Fine," he said again.

"Can I walk this time?" I said as Clarissa loped easily away. I knew I sounded petulant, but I didn't care. "If it isn't too inconvenient or anything."

That teased a small chuckle out of him, and he looked down at me, seeming to really see me for the first time since he'd set me down. "Why not?"

He held out an elbow, and I blinked at it for a moment before I realized that I was supposed to take it.

Right, then.

I hooked my arm over his, and he walked us—slowly—back to the apartment entrance. Compared to the djinn, his presence was almost reassuring, the spike of attraction that ran through me every time we touched familiar and, if not manageable, at least not an ugly surprise.

And that was an indication of just how crazy my life had gotten, I thought. Worth had put my keys into the purse she had given me, and I fished them out and slid my keycard in the door. It unlocked, and Dorian reached past me to pull the door open.

"So, do you care to explain all that?" I asked as we crossed to the lobby elevator and I punched the button to go up.

"What part did you miss?" he returned.

"Clarissa's device let her see the invisible djinn," I said. "And then *she* went half-invisible, and she made him visible. And none of that makes any sense at all."

The elevator arrived, and I stepped in and hit the button for the fourth floor.

"Djinn can move between dimensions," Dorian said, following me. "'Invisible' is close enough. The cords were soaked in salt. Salts—all salts, not just table salt—disrupt their ability to shift between dimensions. They disrupt most of their abilities, actually. Many salts work better than the usual sodium chloride, but table salt is plentiful, relatively cheap, and easy to handle. That's why humans used to think that salt brought good luck. Most of their superstitions didn't do anything, of course, but a circle of salt around a building was—and is—an excellent precaution."

"And that's not magic," I said.

"Not at all," he said, oblivious to my sarcasm. "It's the strongly ionic bonds—there has to be a certain level of slip to allow the djinn to use their interdimensional skills, and the charge of the ions interferes. It drops them right out of phase."

"Of course it does." I gave up. "But I saw the other djinn coming—the one who attacked me."

His expression was hard. "Djinn are known for their…interesting sense of humor. It's their most common failing. She must have been playing with you. It cost her dearly."

The elevator doors opened on the fourth floor, and Dorian led the way out. At my door, he held out his hand. More paranoia, I hoped, but I gave my keys over. If there were interdimensional assassins around, I'd prefer to err on the side of caution, too.

He unlocked the door, pushing it open and moving quickly through the apartment. I waited at the door.

"It's clear," he said.

"I'll only be a moment." I entered, peeling off my coat and shoving my sunglasses in the pocket before hanging it on one of the hooks behind the door. Then I paused, frowning.

The room smelled wrong, the scent of a piney cleaner in the air. My roommates and I had split up the shopping list at the beginning of the year. Lisette had bought the broom, dustpan, sponges, and rags; Chelsea had bought the dishwashing soap and paper towels; Christina had stocked up on toilet paper; and I had bought the cleaning supplies—lemon-scented, like what my Gramma had always used.

Someone else had been here. The carpet was freshly vacuumed, and even from the other side of the peninsula, I could see that the stove and microwave had been scrubbed until they gleamed. I stepped into my room, which was in a perpetual state of clutter from the boxes from my Gramma's house I had stashed there, lacking any other place to put them. The pile of laundry that had overflowed the hamper before finals was gone, and even the boxes had been dusted. I opened the top drawer of my dresser and found my clothes neatly washed and folded inside.

I glared at a pair of socks. I could accept the attack that had nearly taken my life. I could—almost—wrap my mind around the bond that Dorian claimed tied me to him, at least as an alternative to death. I could even be grateful that he had fixed my car since it was ultimately his fault that it had been damaged.

But this was a step too far.

I stepped back into the main living area. Dorian was peering between two slats of the mini blinds, the light glinting off his sunglasses. He looked out of place in my apartment, elegantly attired in his oxford cloth shirt and designer shoes, standing next to the university-issued couch and the one from my Gramma's house that I'd squeezed in at a right angle. An unmistakable vampire.

He didn't belong here. My apartment couldn't be farther from his world. Somehow, I could accept a djinn on the sidewalk more easily than Dorian in the middle of my living room.

"I told you that I was going to clean my apartment," I said.

He turned around, letting the blinds snap closed and slipping his sunglasses into the pocket of his coat he'd folded over the back of the nearest chair with the shoulder holster that he'd been wearing.

"I didn't want you to worry about it."

"I wasn't *worrying*. I was planning." I struggled to find words that didn't make me sound stupid or childish. "Look, I had a life before you came around. It was a nice life."

His eyes narrowed. "It was going to be a short one."

I snapped. "It was the life I wanted to save! *That* was the life that I wanted. It was going to school, hanging out with my friends—cleaning toilets. Yeah, that was part of it, too. Maybe that part wasn't fun, maybe it wasn't something to look forward to, but it was part of my life, and you had no business sending someone to come in here and—and—*fix* it. Going through my things. Changing everything around."

Dorian went very still during my tirade, his gaze fixed upon me. I didn't know if I'd just made him angry. I wished I didn't care. I stood in the doorway, my entire body poised, though I didn't know for what.

Something between a shrug and a shudder went through him. He closed the distance between us, threading trough the jumble of furniture to stop a scant foot away from me. My body ached with his nearness, longing for his touch, but I didn't move, setting my jaw and meeting his pale eyes steadily.

"I meant it as a gift, Cora," he said.

I shook my head. "I know. That makes it worse."

"It doesn't have to. You must have some idea of the life that I offer you."

I could only imagine. The finest of everything: houses, cars, clothes, food. I would live practically forever, always young, always strong—as long as one of his enemies didn't get to me. I'd never have to work another day in my life. My sole job would be to…be his.

And all I had to give up was myself. Everything I'd ever wanted would be irrelevant. Everything I'd ever been.

I was to be a placeholder. He'd told me as much the night before. I was a body to fulfill a role, no longer Cora Shaw but Dorian Thorne's cognate.

"I don't want that life, Dorian. I want mine."

"It will be yours. Whatever you imagine—it can all be yours," he said.

I sighed. He didn't understand. He probably couldn't understand. "But I'll never be free."

"Do you really want to be?"

He was so close now. I couldn't think with him looking at me like that. I closed my eyes. "Free" meant that he would never—*could* never touch me again, like he had. It meant that I would never again feel the way he made me feel because there was no way, without the things he did to my mind, for a human body to feel like that.

"Yes. No. I don't know."

My eyes flew open as his hand cupped my chin, his thumb feather-light across my lips. He bent down and kissed me softly, his mouth moving slowly over mine as he gathered me into his arms.

I came to him, hungry for him, as I always was. Warmth rippled out from my center, making my head boozy and my limbs heavy. I hooked my arms around his neck, pulling his head down to meet mine, inviting him to kiss me deeper.

He did, taking my mouth, pulling my body against his, his hands sliding across my butt and up under the edge of my shirt against my skin.

He pulled back, still holding me to him, and rested

his forehead against mine. I could feel the tension thrumming through his body and into mine.

I said, "None of this should be real. That's the problem. You shouldn't be here."

It was probably one of the dumbest things I'd ever said, but I meant it. Nothing that had happened since I first stepped foot in Dorian's house should have been a part of my well-ordered world. I should have walked in, gotten a cure, and walked out, unaltered except for the cancer.

Instead, I'd been thrust into another life and my own had been stolen away.

"The world hasn't changed, Cora. It's just much bigger and much more complicated than you ever imagined it to be."

There was a quote that teased at the edge of my mind, something that I'd read in high school English class. *There are more things in heaven and earth, Horatio, than are dreamt of in your philosophy....* That wasn't it, but it was close.

Of course, Hamlet went crazy in the end, or pretended he was crazy until there really was no difference. Reassuring thought.

Impulsively, I threaded my fingers through Dorian's short hair. "I don't want complicated. I want...happy."

"You don't imagine that I can make you happy?"

Oh, God, he was beautiful, beautiful and alien, and he wanted me. And all I wanted was for him to kiss me again and never stop.

But I said, "Is it happiness when you don't have a

choice? I don't love you. I know I don't, because it's just not possible. But without you, I'm afraid I might die."

"You won't ever be without me," he said, and the world seemed to slide sideways as he kissed me again.

He moved toward my bedroom, but I didn't want him there. I turned us back toward the living room.

"We'd better make it fast," I managed. "Or someone might come up to investigate." I didn't care, and I didn't want it or anything to be fast, but I felt like I had an obligation to remind him, since I didn't know what kind of personal or political fallout there would be if he left the others cooling their heels for too long.

"Not *too* fast," he said with a smile that could only be described as feral.

And then his mouth met my neck, and nothing else mattered. I stopped thinking, let it all go, gave myself over to him. My skin came alive at his touch, demanding that there be nothing between us. His lips sent sharp, liquid heat driving down between my legs, craving him, needing him.

My hands collided with his as we worked at our clothes—shirts, shoes, pants and underwear, and finally my bra, which ended up hooked over the sink faucet after my too-enthusiastic toss. The heat in my center was wound tight, as if I would break, pulling every nerve until it hummed with the tension. He urged me onto the institutional sofa, and I half-sat, half-tumbled onto it.

I lay back against the cushions and burst out laughing. I couldn't help it. It was all too strange and confusing and far too real, more real than anything I had ever felt before. The upholstery rasped my over-sensitive skin, the smell of pine cleaner burning in my nostrils. Even the light in the room seemed brighter, everything picked out in harsh highlights and shadows. I was present, in this moment, as I'd never been present before, and it was bewildering.

How I wanted him—my bones hurt with it, my brain burned, my skin longed for the feeling of his body against mine. I was helpless against it, but a part of me could recognize how absurd it all was. Dorian was something out of legend, and here I was, just...me. And he wanted me—the ageless vampire, the deathless demigod.

But the ridiculousness of it didn't change a thing.

I looked up at Dorian, standing over me, and my laughter died in my throat. His gaze was so keen I thought it could cut me, every contour of his perfect body picked out by the light that filtered in through the blinds. I could feel him pulsing with power, slow, steady beats like his heart.

My gaze was drawn irresistibly to the evidence of his arousal, then snapped back up again to his face as I realized that I was staring. I remembered how he had been the night before, at the limit of his control, rough and demanding and just a hairbreadth from stepping over the edge and taking me with him, down into his darkness....

He said, "I am patience itself, Cora. I do not rush in. I wait decades, centuries, until the time is right. But you—you make me forget myself. Yet I won't hurt you today, Cora. Don't be afraid."

Forget myself. I swallowed. What a perfect phrase

for what I was afraid was happening to me. I was forgetting myself, so that I would wake up one morning and be someone completely different.

He put one hand on the couch on either side of my head and bent to take my lips. I thrilled at the touch, soft and hard at once, coaxing and demanding. With a quiet noise, I tilted my head up to meet his kiss, my hands reaching out to skim down across the hard planes of his chest to tighten on his hips, pulling him toward me. He came, and he eased down with me onto the sofa, his mouth moving across my body, teasing the curve of my neck and tracing the line of my collarbone.

Dorian's mouth was insistent on my skin, driving me deeper into the welter of sweet heat that poured over me. When he took my nipple, my entire body shuddered, and my hands tightened on his back. His hand moved down, sliding between my legs to find my clitoris, working in rhythm with his mouth until I was panting and arching against him, my thighs wet with my need.

He slid up my body, between my knees. My legs locked around him, urging him toward me, and he came to me. I hissed as he slid into me, filling me until I panted under his weight. He was moving, taking the same rhythm as before, his hand between us as I rocked with him, faint noises pulled from my throat with every stroke. The heat rose around me, crackling across my skin, rushing in my head, driving into my bones.

I pushed toward the peak, reaching for it with everything in my body until I hit it and I fell, hard, into the swift madness that washed everything else away—

everything but him, taking me, claiming me, plundering my body and piercing my soul.

Dorian shuddered as I came back to earth again, speaking low and fervently in a language I didn't understand until, slowly, he came to rest. He held me against his body for a very long moment, his arms iron bands around me, and I realized with a sudden shock that I was running my fingers through his hair, over and over.

I forced my hand to still, and after another minute, he pulled back. I lay stunned against the couch, watching the strong lines of his back and rear as he found his underwear—my personal vampire wore boxer-briefs, I discovered—and his pants.

He'd kept his word. He hadn't hurt me, not at all.

The slight edge of disappointment I felt at that thought sent a spiral of fear deep into my gut. I bit my lip. Slowly, I pushed up off the couch and gathered the clothes I'd been wearing. I made a brief stop in my bedroom to pick out a new outfit from my own wardrobe—instead of the one Dorian had bought for me—then grabbed the chartreuse purse and ducked into the bathroom.

Avoiding my reflection, I cleaned up and dressed quickly, pausing just long enough to down a pill from the pack in my purse.

Better late than never, right?

I wasn't ashamed of what I'd done. I was afraid of what I wanted to do. All my priorities had been knocked sideways. I was off-kilter, and I didn't know how to right myself. And I wasn't sure I wanted to, because the list of everything that had happened in the last week should make any sane person's head explode.

When I stepped out, Dorian was lounging on my Gramma's sofa in the living room, without even a ruffle of hair to betray what had just passed between us. At the image of him there, sitting on the couch that had been so much a part of my childhood, my body clenched, and I had a sudden, panicked urge to order him away.

But I said, "Just got to pack a few things."

Back in my bedroom, I pulled an empty duffel bag from the top of the closet. I threw in the clothes I'd been wearing and scooped some of my own clothes from the drawers and closet. I retrieved my toiletries from the freshly scrubbed bathroom, then grabbed my wallet, my laptop, and my graduation photo and shoved them on top. At the last minute, I snagged the tiny stuffed rabbit my roommate Lisette had given me for Christmas and added that, too.

I looked around. There didn't seem to be anything else to take. My childhood memories could stay in their boxes, and all the things I'd packed away for my graduate life were worthless in Dorian's house.

Not that I was staying there long.

Dorian plucked the duffel out of my arms as I stepped back into the living area, slinging it over his shoulder as I put the sunglasses and my own coat on, hooking the one that Worth had given me that morning over my arm along with the purse.

"I'm as ready as I'll ever be," I said.

Ready to return to the vampire's home.

CHAPTER ELEVEN

larissa hopped out lightly as soon as the Escalade rolled to a stop.

"Tomorrow, Cora," she said with a smile I didn't care to interpret, and then she shut the door and disappeared.

The driver got out and moved to open the other door, but Dorian held up a hand, waving the man away. With a small bow, the driver retreated several paces, standing against the tall hollies with his hands folded neatly in front of him.

I gave Dorian a sideways look. What was that all about?

Dorian reached into a pocket of his coat, withdrawing a small, wrapped box. "I was reminded that it has become customary for gifts to be exchanged on Christmas Day."

"But I didn't get you anything," I protested as I took it out of reflex.

Like what? I wondered. Did vampires like cufflinks and tie clips? Expensive cologne? I couldn't imagine that I could afford any sort of appropriate gift for him—even if I wanted to give him something. And I wasn't sure that I did. You gave friends presents, or boyfriends. Dorian didn't fit into any of those neat categories.

"I had no expectation that you would," he said.

My stomach tightened slightly. Yet another debt I would owe him.

"Really, I don't think it's appropriate," I said, pressing it back toward him.

"You can at least open it before refusing it." He spoke quietly, but I felt the will behind his words, and I couldn't resist.

I wondered if he could hear it, too—if he even knew what he was doing to me. Reluctantly, I popped the heavy wrapping paper open with my thumb where it was taped. Inside was a plain white box, and inside that was a velvet jewelry case.

Oh, damn.

What else would it be, really, following custom, as he said?

I opened the case cautiously. Even in the dimmed light coming through the tinted windows, the faceted ruby glittered darkly, a single perfect pear nestled into a curving gold teardrop pendant that perfectly matched the mark on the inside of my wrist. I wasn't sure how many carats it was—way too many, was all I knew, and I was certain that it was real.

The message was inescapable. It was a declaration of our bond, that I now belonged to him, and an unsubtle reminder of his wealth and all of the material comfort he could offer me.

A necklace might be an appropriate gift, maybe, considering that we did have a relationship, however unconventional. But this was simply too much, too soon, too expensive. And yet it was so clearly mine, made for no one but me, so obviously personal that the extravagance of it was less significant than the intimate intention.

It wasn't an intimacy that I wanted. I thought of everything that had passed between us, and I shivered. How much more intimate could two people be?

"I can't accept this," I said.

"Everything I have is now yours," he said.

I looked at him askance and realized that he meant it. I shook my head. "Except that it's not. It's *really* not. It's mine as far as you want to share it—and not one bit farther. No matter what you give me, it's only mine as far as I'm yours. And I don't want that." I pressed the box back into his hands, careful not to touch his skin.

He didn't take it. "Then don't keep it for yourself. Keep it as something to wear at your introduction. Something to keep in the jewelry box in the room at my house—that is also not yours, if you wish to see it that way."

Crap. The introduction. I hadn't thought about it in

hours. It was another one of those things that didn't seem quite real.

He opened the vehicle door and offered me his arm. My mind churning, I took it and slid out, the shiver of attraction at our contact muddling my head even more. The driver jumped over to the rear hatch and got my duffle bag. The cheap, rumpled canvas looked ridiculous in his white-gloved hands.

"What, exactly, is this introduction?" I asked, shifting the purse on my shoulder. "I mean, I know it introduces me into your vampire society and everything. But I don't know what any of that *means*."

He arched an eyebrow, guiding the way up the stone walk to the house. "You should know that vampire is a human word, not the one that we prefer. It is considered by some to be a pejorative."

The thought of vampires getting offended at the name that humans used for them struck me as absurd.

"Well, vampires don't exactly have an excellent reputation," I said acidly. "Maybe it's the whole killing people thing that's caused all the irrational stereotypes. That kind of behavior does tend to upset people."

"Indeed," Dorian said, pressing his lips together as if he were suppressing a smile.

Eating people shouldn't be funny. It really shouldn't. But I was tired and stressed, and my head was beginning to hurt, and I couldn't help the thin thread of a giggle that emerged. I relaxed fractionally despite myself. Despite everything.

"The introduction is just a brief ceremony," Dorian said, serious again. "It formalizes your place as my cognate, offering you certain protections and privileges."

"What am I supposed to wear?" I asked. My hand tightened for a moment around the jewelry box. If he expected me to wear that, it must be pretty damn formal. "I've still got my prom dress," I offered, somewhat weakly.

I thought about the kind of clothes the impeccable Dorian and glamorous Clarissa would wear to a formal event. Yeah, my prom dress, which changed from a shimmering tangerine to a bright pink, depending on the angle, wouldn't look totally ridiculous next to them.

Sure.

"Worth has already taken care of that," Dorian said.

I wanted to protest. I'd already been forced by necessity to wear his clothes once. I didn't really want to make a habit of it. It made my protests about his gifts seem pretty stupid when I was constantly using the things I said I didn't want.

But on the other hand…it was his party, set up for his benefit in his society. Why should I have to look absurd or spend money I really didn't have? Forget my student loans—I didn't even know how I was going to pay for my apartment through the next semester with the out-of-pocket medical expenses that I owed.

"Fine," I said, stopping at the top of the stairs in front of the great double doors. "I'll wear whatever Worth comes up with. And I'll wear the necklace, too—just this once. And after that, no one is going to try to kill me anymore, right? That's the deal. I go out, I smile at people, and they stop sending interdimensional killers after me."

This time, Dorian did smile. "That sums it up nicely. And now I'm going to wish you a good evening. I should not have spent so much time with you these past two days, but I needed—" He broke off, and I saw a fleeting expression, something I couldn't name, through a brief crack in his impassive façade before it closed over again. "It has been a very long time."

"Are you going back to Baltimore?" I asked with a pang I didn't care to examine.

"It will be for the last night," he said.

Gladness warred with fear—once he no longer felt like he must limit his contact with me, would he ever let me go home again? And if he didn't, what would become of me?

He reached out and brushed my cheek. Instinctively, I leaned into his touch.

"I will be back before the introduction," he said. "I promise."

The butler opened the doors then, and Dorian pressed a brief kiss on my cheek and was gone.

Worth was waiting for me in the bedroom—my bedroom, I finally allowed myself to admit. She put aside her tablet and eyed my outfit with obvious displeasure, her frown deepening when she took in my duffel bag as well. I had taken it very firmly from the driver in the foyer instead of allowing the butler to order a footman to get it—Seriously, a footman! Who besides Cinderella has actual footmen?—and had taken it upstairs myself.

And immediately regretted it, because it had been instantly obvious that I had offended all three. Now, from Worth's expression, I could make it four.

Awesome start, Cora. Let's see if you can piss off all the rest of Dorian's employees.

"I'm sorry that the wardrobe is not to your tastes, m—Cora," she said in a voice that managed to be haughty and subservient at the same time. I was beginning to suspect that her accidents with my name were nothing of the sort.

I dropped the duffel on the bed with a sigh. "The clothes are gorgeous, Worth." I shook my head. "Gah, I can't keep calling you that. What's your first name?"

"Jane," she said frostily.

"Jane," I repeated. "Everything you picked out is amazing. I don't even know how you could find things that fit so well, considering that I didn't even try them on. But they're not mine. I know my clothes are boring and not really fashionable—"

Jane Worth made a noise that implied that this was the understatement of the century.

"—*But* they are mine. Target and Forever 21 and Old Navy. That's what I have, okay? I don't want to wear what Dorian's paid for." I remembered the introduction the next day. "Well, at least not if I can help it,"

I finished lamely.

"Mr. Thorne wants you to have the best," she said, an accusation in her voice, as if it were a personal failing to want something other than what Dorian desired.

To her, it probably was.

"I know, Jane," I said. "And I know that you probably spent hours putting together a wardrobe that could cover every possible clothing need." From her flinch, I knew I was right. "And I appreciate it. I really do. But it's not really mine. Can't you see that?"

"Yes, Cora," she said.

It didn't sound convincing.

Great, I thought. *Now my lady's maid hates me. And I don't even want a lady's maid.*

"Would m—you care for dinner?" the woman asked.

"That sounds wonderful," I said, glad I could do something that she would approve of. "But the chef doesn't need to go all-out or anything, like he has been. Really. I mostly eat ramen and mac and cheese and spaghetti when I don't eat dorm food, so I don't need to be pampered."

"You don't like what he's been serving?" I could have gotten frostbite from her tone.

Crap. How the hell had I walked into that?

I backtracked desperately. "No, no! I love it. It's the best food anyone has ever made for me. I just don't want to be a bother."

"It is our job to see that you have the best of everything," Jane said. "Our job is not a *bother.*"

"Of course not. Have him send up whatever he

wants," I agreed hastily.

"Indeed, madam," she said, the honorific sliding out almost like an insult to my overly sensitized ears.

Jane tapped for a moment on her phone, then took my duffel bag into the closet. I flopped onto an upholstered chair and stared out the window over the roof and into the back garden, wondering how I would even be able to eat around the foot in my mouth.

I felt sorry for myself. I wasn't proud of it, but all I wanted was to hide away in the room by myself and have a private little pity-party. Instead, I was painfully reminded of how many other people were affected by my new position.

It wasn't a comfortable thought. All my life, there had only been me and Gramma, and in the past year, just me. Sure, I had friends, but they didn't really depend on me for anything. Whether I did great or screwed up, I was the only one it really mattered to. My friends were sympathetic, but their lives weren't enmeshed with mine.

It was different here. As Dorian's cognate, my very existence had a meaning so great that someone wanted me dead. And Dorian's household was set up to revolve around two points, the lesser one very clearly being me.

I was more important that I'd ever imagined being…but at the same time, my own identity was completely irrelevant to that importance. Any other female who bonded to Dorian would be in the exact same role.

I didn't owe Jane anything. How could I? But just the same, she'd been working for years toward the eventual goal of working for Dorian's cognate. Who happened to be me. So when I showed up, it should have been the fulfillment of all her ambitions. It should have been a justification for her taking a job that might never have had a real purpose.

Instead, I was messing with all her expectations, refusing all the things that she saw as the point of her career.

In short, I was a big, fat jerk.

I closed my eyes and groaned aloud.

"Are you quite all right?" Jane materialized in the doorway.

"I'm fine," I said with determined cheer. "Thanks so much for putting my things away."

"Not a problem," she said, looking slightly mollified.

I took a deep breath, ready to try to navigate the rocky conversational waters with my new lady's maid. "I've probably never been to anything as fancy as this introduction. High school formals aren't really the same, are they? I'm going to entirely depend on you for everything—clothes, hair, makeup." I remembered the necklace and pulled its case out of my pocket. "Dorian gave me this. He thought you might want to use it."

Jane took it from my hand and flipped open the lid. She sniffed. "He should leave dressing a lady to me. I suppose I could work it in."

"Whatever you think is best," I said, happy enough to have an ally, however unlikely, against the gift. Whatever sense of loyalty Dorian required of her, it clearly didn't exclude all criticism, and I was grateful to have

110

some of her scorn directed somewhere else.

"I've already picked out your dress, if it meets with your satisfaction," Jane added, in a tone that implied that any reasonable person would believe that it would.

"I've seen your taste, and I know it will," I said firmly.

At that point, I would have worn a potato sack if I thought it'd make her happy. Was that stupid? Probably. But I didn't have the energy to spare for a battle of wills with the lady's maid that I didn't even want.

"What happened to all the flowers, anyway?" I asked. The enormous, cloying bouquets no longer crowded every surface. Instead, there were now only two vases with much more modest displays.

"Oh, did you like them all?" Jane looked chagrined.

"Uh…" I didn't quite know what to say. *Yes,* and I was certain the room would soon be full to bursting—*no,* and I might insult her. "I was just curious. There seemed to be…so many of them," I finished lamely.

"They were congratulatory presents," Worth said. "Sent by other cognates and by agnates who had no cognates. You'll get more, after the introduction, of course, but these were all unofficial, sent by Mr. Thorne's very closest allies."

Allies, I noticed. Not *friends.* Did vampires have friends?

"And I was supposed to be a secret?" I said aloud. "There must have been a dozen of them!"

"Thereabouts," she agreed. "But they'd never say a word about it. They wouldn't even let their staff know. Most of our own staff didn't know. Most were sent away as soon as it became clear that your conversion would work. In fact, today is the first day everyone's back at work."

"Oh," I said, still thinking that telling a dozen people was a pretty sorry way of keeping a secret.

Jane just smiled before disappearing into the dressing room with the velvet box. She reappeared holding my laptop, my graduation photo, and Nibbler.

"Where do you want these, Cora?" For the first time, my name didn't have a bite in it.

I cast around. "The desk for the laptop, if there's a wall socket nearby, and the bedside table for the rest."

I had to suppress a giggle at the solemn way in which Worth arranged the tiny stuffed rabbit in front of the framed picture, as if she were trying to find the angle at which it looked the most appealing among the elegant décor of the room.

They were such little things—the picture in its plastic frame and the stupid little toy. But seeing them there made me smile, and for the first time, I felt like there was a place for me in the room.

Almost like I belonged.

And that thought made me shiver all over again.

CHAPTER TWELVE

After breakfast the next morning, I curled up in a chair with my laptop, nursing the headache I'd had since the evening before. Jane had suggested that I look around the house and grounds.

"You are its mistress, after all," she had said, managing, as usual, to find just the wrong words to make me feel at ease.

But I'd begun to feel at least somewhat at home in my corner of the vast house, so I'd declined. The bedroom that Dorian had selected for his cognate was as big as my entire campus apartment—bigger, even, if you included the bathroom and dressing room—so I hardly felt cooped up.

A dining area took up one section of the room, complete with a circular table with four chairs around it and a sideboard against the wall, and a corner by the windows boasted a sitting area with small sofa—a settee, really—and an overstuffed chair that was perfect for curling up with one of the throws that were scattered about. Of course, when I'd done that, contently ensconced with the blanket around my shoulders, Jane had come fluttering in, asking, "Are you sure you're not cold?"

There was even a small work area with a desk and a bookcase. I imagined that it had been intended for the lady of the house to spend hours every day going over her longhand correspondence or something equally refined and outdated.

In truth, I didn't want to wander around the house by myself. It wasn't that I didn't feel curious. The idea just made me feel like an intruder—whatever Jane said, I was certain in my mind that I wasn't anyone's or anything's mistress. And I was still more than a little wary of what else might be in the house, besides overly eager staff members whom I accidentally offended at every turn.

So I sent Jane away as politely as possible and hid out in my room, surfing the internet, reading the newest bestseller Hannah had told me I just had to try, and messaging my friends on Facebook.

Until Geoff's name lit with a green dot, and a moment later, a message popped up.

You said it went well. Good to hear.

I blinked. Oh, God, Geoff. What on earth was I supposed to say to Geoff?

Yeah. I'm feeling pretty great, I typed back.

That was safe.

The typing message flashed—for far longer than it should. He was writing, then erasing, then writing again.

Finally, the message arrived. *Wonderful. Can't wait to see you next semester.*

I let out a breath of air. Next semester. Geoff and I had gone out on one date—right before I'd gotten my cancer diagnosis. It had been nice. Well, it had been more than nice, and I'd been looking forward to that date turning into something steadier.

But once I found out about my cancer, everything had changed. Sure, we'd had an on-again, off-again mutual crush for a couple of years, but there didn't seem to be a good opening for saying, "Hey, yeah, being your girlfriend would be great, and by the way, I'm probably going to die. Hope that's okay!"

Eventually, my roommate Lisette had told him about my cancer, and he'd made it clear that he was still interested in me. By that point, I'd decided to take the treatment that Dorian had offered, knowing only that it would either cure me or kill me.

So I had told Geoff that if I was feeling better after the Winter Break, we'd give a relationship a real shot.

Of course, I hadn't counted on being bonded for life to an ageless vampire, much less ending up in his bed.

Yeah. Complications.

But Geoff was…still Geoff. And I realized that whatever I felt for Dorian, if it could even be named, existed separately from what I felt for Geoff. My feelings for Geoff were familiar, comforting—and altogether human. He was a reminder of what my dreams had always been, the boyfriend, the degree, the career, the house, and eventually, the kids. The picture-perfect life that would show my Gramma that everything she'd done for me was worth it.

Plus, I wouldn't say that his touch wasn't quite pleasant in its way—hell, sometimes way more than pleasant—but it couldn't drive me to insanity. I never imagined that I wanted him to hurt me. And that was always a bonus.

I'm looking forward to it, too, I typed.

Eh. Stiff and awkward enough, Cora? But it got the point across.

The message alert sounded. *Cool.*

Just then, the door opened, and Jane entered, carrying another tray overloaded with food.

Quickly, I wrote, *GTG,* and I closed the lid of the laptop.

"I've got lunch," Jane announced with a smile, setting the tray on the center of the table.

I suppressed a groan as I stood up. I thought I'd eaten enough for three meals at breakfast.

"And after that, it will be time to get ready for the introduction," she added.

"What's it like?" I asked.

"Oh, we've never had one before, so I don't truly know. But the butler and the housekeeper and the event planner have been having fits for days, so it's got to be impressive," she said with barely contained excitement.

Ah, Jane. So skilled at saying the exact thing I didn't want to hear.

I tucked into my food obediently, my reluctance

evaporating with the first taste. As soon as I set my spoon and fork down with a sigh—would I ever be happy with mac and cheese again?—Jane herded me into the dressing room to start the process of transforming me into an image fit to be Dorian's cognate.

It was four hours before the beginning of the gala. I wondered if she'd have enough time.

"The gown!" Jane announced with a dramatic wave of her hand.

It hung from a hook in front of the closet, turned outward so that it could be seen in its full glory. The dress was, without question, gorgeous. A shimmery, ethereal green, it was strapless, with a sweetheart neckline made of many-pleated wrapped layers in a figure-hugging bodice that went down to the hips and met a tight skirt that flared out in a mermaid's tail at the knees. It was covered in intricate beadwork that was as subtle as it was extravagant.

"It's stunning," I said, feeling a little dismayed. "And it's built for curves that, at the moment, I don't have." The cancer had not been kind to my body, and though I no longer looked like the survivor of a death camp, I had at least five pounds to go before I moved from looking half-starved to merely too thin.

Jane smiled and pulled out a foundation garment that looked like something out of the Gilded Age. "And that, madam, is why we cheat."

I was clearly outmatched, and I submitted myself to her with good grace. I couldn't see how corsetry could possibly make me look less thin—until the garment was on and cinched tightly enough that I considered cracking a *Gone with the Wind* joke.

But then I looked in the mirror, and I understood. My waist was not merely smaller—the corset had a generous amount of padding that reshaped the lines of my hips and breasts.

"I think this is called false advertising," I said, looking at the artificial curves in bemusement.

"It is called enhancement," Jane corrected. Her tone was prim, but her eyes danced with pleasure.

She helped me wrestle the dress over my head, tugging and pulling it into place. The effect was gorgeous. There was really no other word for it. My arms still looked a little too thin, my collarbones a trifle too prominent, but it was otherwise perfect.

"Excellent. Just a little *here*, and it will be perfect." Jane pronounced her professional judgment as she quickly used a few pins to change a seam that was puckering slightly. "Of course, only if you agree, madam," she added with perfunctory subservience.

"I think I have to," I said, staring at myself.

"Very good." She eyed my nails. "Dress and foundation garments off again, then manicure, hair, and cosmetics."

I obeyed and found myself wrapped in a fluffy white robe and hustled over to the dressing table chair, where she trimmed and shaped my short nails and covered them with a pale, glossy pink polish. As they dried, my hair was curled and teased and smoothed again, then pinned and sprayed until it had the careless perfection that could only be achieved with enormous amounts of effort, tumbling from a mass at the top of my head to brush the nape of my neck. Then she attacked my nails again, spreading some kind of cream on them as she buffed each one carefully to a high shine.

Jane nodded in satisfaction, then attacked my face with equal enthusiasm. I winced as she shaped my eyebrows, something I hadn't gotten around to in months. Then came a battery of cosmetic products—concealer, foundation, highlight and lowlight contours, powder, then brow pencil, eye shadow, eyeliner on the waterline and lashline, mascara, individual false eyelashes, blush, lip conditioner, lip liner, lipstick, and gloss.

When she finally allowed me to look at myself, I braced for all the horrors of a drag queen. But the reality was startling. After half an hour of fussing and painting, I looked like...myself. Only better. Peculiarly, I looked like I was wearing less makeup than I did when I applied my own.

"That shouldn't actually be possible," I said, peering at my reflection.

"Clever little pots of paint, aren't they, Cora?" Jane beamed over my shoulder.

"I think it has more to do with the hand holding the brush than the makeup itself," I said, thinking of the mess I'd make of it if I tried to apply all those products to myself.

"Mmmm," was all Jane said, but I could tell she liked the compliment. "Jewelry," she said. "And scent. Though neither need be applied until just before the event."

She brought out a parade of perfumes. I recognized Chanel No. 5, but the others I had never heard of—

Ralph Lauren's Notorious, Shalimar, Caron's Poivre, Joy by Jean Patou, and more that I could not even remember the names of. After smelling half a dozen on tester strips, I gave up and waved them away.

"I can't smell anything straight anymore," I said. "You pick one. You were right on the hair, dress, and makeup. You'll probably do a better job of selecting a perfume, too."

"Very good, Cora," she said, practically preening with smugness as she slid the tray away. "And now for jewelry."

From a black velvet box came a necklace just a little longer than a choker made of oval-cut emeralds placed end to end in a gold setting, along with a matching bracelet and a set of earrings. The ruby pendant had been taken from the necklace that Dorian had given me to be worked into the center of the emeralds.

"You approve?" Jane asked.

"Of course," I said, not even attempting to calculate its value.

"Mr. Thorne would like to speak to you before the party," Jane said, offering me a pair of slippers. "He will be having a light tea in his study."

I put the slippers on. Always, there was someone waiting for me now. It was a strange sensation—I was much more used to waiting than being waited on, in any sense of the word.

"Well, then," I said. "I suppose I should go and see him."

And once again, I was led to Dorian.

CHAPTER THIRTEEN

When Jane opened the door to the mezzanine, a cacophony of voices and banging almost drove me back inside. I hesitated in the doorway before carefully stepping out to look over the railing into the salon below.

And then I really did have to stop myself from running back into my bedroom.

The salon teemed. Dozens of people crisscrossed the room, men in sharp black suits threading their way among various tradesmen. Some were carting in great armloads of flowers. Others carried screens, urns, and statues, even rolling in ice sculptures and fountains. Pacing around the chaos, a woman with a tablet and a notebook snapped orders as she orchestrated the group-ings of furniture into a different configuration. At her direction, two men rolled out a long red carpet from the foot of one leg of the stairs all the way to the center of the room in front of a massive object that reached halfway to the ceiling, hidden under a black drape.

My heart beat a little faster. The introduction had not seemed quite real before—it was hard to imagine the echoing mausoleum of a mansion filled with light and noise and people. Now the immediacy of it settled over me, and I realized that the scale of it was beyond anything I'd imagined. I would be standing with Dorian in that room soon, facing how many agnates I couldn't even guess, including, quite possibly, more than one who wanted me dead.

What had I gotten myself into?

Clarissa and another agnate stood on either side of my door—more guards, I realized, just to make sure that I was safe amid the bustle of preparations. Clarissa shot me a grin.

"Just keeping you in one piece until the party," she said brightly. "But there's nothing to worry about. More of Dorian's paranoia."

Right.

The other agnate didn't even acknowledge me, but they both fell in behind me as Worth led the way downstairs, stepping carefully around the runner to the colonnade passageway. I padded behind her in my robe with the guards following. No one seemed to notice me. It seemed strange to be so invisible since the introduction was, at least supposedly, all about me.

I guessed that I would only matter once I came out to play my part, an actor in a set piece.

"The mistress, Mr. Thorne," Worth announced

sententiously as she opened the door to the study that Dorian had interviewed her in two nights before.

"I'm nobody's *mistress*," I said automatically as I stepped inside.

At my entrance, Dorian stood and crossed the room to meet me, his hair perfectly combed as always, a smile of greeting on his inhumanly handsome face. My breath felt squeezed in my chest. He was wearing suit pants and a matching vest with a real-life smoking jacket over it. It had a deep cowl collar, silk tassels, and everything.

The sight of him brought back a too-vivid flood of memories—his mouth on mine, his hands moving across my naked body, me writhing beneath him as he filled me—

His expression left no shadow of doubt that his mind was in the same place when he looked at me.

I shook my head to clear it and then said, lightly, "Channeling Hugh Hefner?"

"What?" He followed my gaze downward, then scowled. "I'll have you know that the smoking jacket was the preferred loungewear of gentlemen long before that panderer corrupted it."

A tiny giggle escaped me, and he looked up sharply. His eyes narrowed with the realization that I was teasing. I got the sense that he wasn't used to anyone joking with him in that way.

He put on an expression of mock sternness. "And what does the wardrobe of a woman of your elevated sartorial sense look like?"

"You've pretty much seen it. Mostly jeans and yoga pants and t-shirts," I admitted. "Some sweaters and sweatshirts, too, for variety."

Dorian hooked his arm in mine in the easy, old-fashioned mannerism that he had, and a shiver went through me. It was so peculiar, like something out of a movie, that it should have felt awkward. But it didn't. I was with him again, breathing the air of the same room, touching him, if only through our clothing. My body prickled with a glad awareness, my breath coming quicker despite my attempt at self-control.

He led me to the leather sofa, positioned between the two club chairs that Jane and I had occupied two nights before. I sat at one end, cautiously. He took a seat diagonally against the wide arm, hooking a leg up onto the cushion between us with careless grace.

"You must keep the tabloids busy," he said.

I shook my head ruefully at the memory of the djinn Finnegan and his camera. "I guess I do, if Finnegan's got any company. Are there such things as vampire tabloids?"

"There are underground presses of various sorts," Dorian admitted. "But you don't go to the papers for the truth. If you want to know the real news, you have to be among the people who create it."

"And you're one of those." It wasn't a question.

"Of course."

"Today—this introduction is going to be news, too," I said. "Because of your research."

"Yes. There will be much gnashing of teeth among my enemies."

My smile was tight. I knew that Dorian had meant

that as a light sort of joke, but given that we were talking about vampires, the figure of speech made me just a little queasy.

"Do you approve of Worth's efforts?" he asked after a moment, his wave encompassing my hair and makeup.

"Whatever you're paying her, it's not enough," I said fervently.

He fell silent again, and I fidgeted, knotting my hands in my lap. There must be something important, something he'd decided to tell me, or else he wouldn't have called me down here just before the party. However good his staff was, there must have been a hundred other things for him to do.

But he just propped one hand under his chin, tracing the aquiline bridge of his own nose with his eyebrows drawn together in a way I had begun to recognize as unease.

I waited, shifting uncomfortably, afraid of what he didn't want to say.

Abruptly, he motioned to the coffee table, which was set with a tray with various pots and arrayed with a variety of finger foods. "Tea? Coffee?"

It was an offer to fill the silence between us, the closest that he had ever come to betraying uncertainty around me.

"Thanks." I hadn't developed the usual college student coffee addiction, so I poured a cup of tea instead.

What could be so awful that he didn't want to tell me? I swallowed too quickly, and the hot tea burnt my tongue and throat, making me cough as I hurriedly set the cup down.

Still, Dorian was silent.

"So. My first vampire party," I said. "I'm hoping that people-eating is not involved." I was joking. Mostly.

"Not in a Lesser Introduction," he said dryly.

I could hear the capital letters, and I frowned as I sipped the tea again—this time with more care.

"I thought that 'lesser' would mean, you know, *less*." I waved toward the door to encompass the preparations that were taking place outside. "That doesn't look like less than any party I've ever been to. Maybe less compared to Times Square at New Year's, or maybe less than some sort of crazy Roman bash where they ate flamingo's tongue and hummingbirds and then threw it all up in a vomitorium before going back for sevenths, but not less compared to the sorts of parties normal people imagine."

That teased a slight smile out of Dorian, the crease between his eyes easing fractionally. "It's not lesser because it's a small party. It's lesser because a Grand Introduction is considered more important. A Lesser Introduction is when a cognate—in this case, you—is formally introduced to agnatic society during a party that generally features a greeting period, a buffet dinner, and dancing."

"Like a debutante ball from hell," I said without thinking.

Dorian ignored the *from hell* part and said, "Almost exactly like a debutante ball, except in this case, the debutante is always already taken."

It was all about me without being about *me* at all. I

again had the sense of being pushed into a blank space that had been waiting for the first person who happened to fit it. It was like a Cinderella story that started with the glass slipper instead of ending with it.

"So what would a Grand Introduction be?" I prompted.

Dorian's expression went very still. "A coming-of-age party for a vampire."

"Coming-of-age?" I asked, making a face over such an archaic phrase.

"When a member of our society is considered to reach full adulthood, which among us is judged to be age forty," he said with equanimity.

"Forty. That's like half a lifetime," I said.

"For humans," Dorian pointed out.

Not for agnates, of course. And not for cognates, either.

I'd seen all too clearly how terrible age could be through my Gramma, as much as she'd tried to hide it. To be spared that, to have a body that would never fail me the way hers had failed her—hell, the way cancer had caused mine to fail me....

Would it really be such a sacrifice? All I would be giving up would be...myself, giving myself over to be shaped to Dorian's will. And after a while, there wouldn't be a single person left in the world who even remembered Cora Shaw, the human. Only what Dorian would turn me into.

The thought of it made a cold, hard knot in the pit of my stomach.

"Point taken," I said.

"Forty is the age at which most vampires must begin to consume human blood," Dorian continued. "It used to be a more…primal ceremony among many of our people. Now it is simply a dinner and dance, not too much different from a Lesser Introduction."

I shuddered, visualizing all too clearly what he meant by *primal*. But even that couldn't prevent the re-emergence of the thought that had kept rising in my mind over the past three days.

"You still haven't told me how vampires are born. And don't try to deflect me this time. It's not going to work," I added, even though I knew it wasn't true.

Dorian looked at me for a long moment, and I realized that this was the information he had summoned me here to tell me all along.

"This you must know before your introduction begins, for you would surely find out during it. Cognates are more than just nourishment and pleasure, Cora."

CHAPTER FOURTEEN

My stomach dropped, and I set my teacup down so hard that some of the hot liquid sloshed over the edge. It wasn't that I didn't suspect. There were only a limited number of answers he might have given, and that was one of them. I'd just refused to allow myself to fully think about that possibility.

Until now.

I put my hands protectively over my midsection. "You told me that I couldn't get pregnant!"

"You can't," he said quickly. "Not yet, at any rate. Not so soon after a bond is formed. It takes years for that part of a conversion to take place—always at least five, often as long as ten."

I glared at him. "I didn't trust you, you know. I went to the Health Center for birth control pills."

"I know. They won't hurt you—give you a head-ache, perhaps—but they won't have any effect on you now, one way or another."

Right. The headache I'd had since taking the first pill yesterday afternoon. "You could have said something."

"Would you have believed me? Do you even believe me now?"

I stopped. He was right. It didn't really make a dif-ference because he had already told me that I couldn't get pregnant, and I hadn't trusted him then—had not trusted my own trust in what he had said.

But now a new thought came to me, the realization slow and terrible. Not only could I get pregnant by him, eventually at least, but any child I had with him would be another vampire. A killer.

All my old dreams seemed to mock me. The job, the house, the husband, the kids....

To be a cognate, tied to Dorian forever, living in his great, cold, echoing mansion and bearing him chil-dren that would grow up to be monsters just like him....

"I won't do it," I said, standing abruptly. "I can't. What kind of person would give birth to a child they'd know would grow up to be a murderer?"

"It's not murder, Cora," he said, looking up at me.

"Yes, because you're not human," I snapped. "I've heard it all before. I don't care. You still kill people to live, a lot of people. And I'm not going to make more of you."

"Do you suppose your existence would be a threat if you didn't?" Dorian said. He hadn't moved, but his casual posture was now belied by the tension in his frame. I could sense the darkness seething around him, wrapped tightly to him as if grasped in an iron control.

I didn't understand him. "What do you mean?"

"*Think*, Cora." His words came out rapidly, like gunfire. "This is a war of ideology, one that I was bound to lose through the tyranny of arithmetic. Those agnates who believe that humans should be used for their pleasure, who give human life no value—they eat whenever they feel the urge, not restricting themselves to what it takes to maintain life and health. So they find cognates, and they have children, children they raise to be like themselves. An agnate who restrains himself would have to live more than two thousand years, on average, to find a cognate. Most of us don't even last that long!"

"So?" I demanded.

"Until you, Cora, our ideology has been doomed to extinction because we cannot reproduce ourselves. To take our stance would be to say that all vampires, everywhere, should eventually die out—and as much as you despise us, that is something very few of us want. And if those of us who share my beliefs die out, there is no one to oppose those who wish to be humanity's rulers. Whatever you think of how agnates live now, how I live, without the agnates like me, it would be a thousand times worse for humans."

The logic was merciless, leading to a single conclusion.

"No," I said, not because he was wrong but because I wanted him to be.

Dorian continued. "But now you're here, proof that there is another way. You promise an end to the killing of humans and also a future life for us. We are born to crave you, Cora. Without a cognate, we are like half a soul. There are agnates who have restrained themselves for hundreds of years, who have gone without that other half because they could not stomach the killing any longer, but it is hard for us, harder than you can believe. And we want children, too, just like every living thing does. We fear our end perhaps even more than humans do because our lives are so much longer, and our children are how we, like you, can make something that continues long after we're gone."

The full and terrible implications sank into my mind.

I was the symbol of his ideology, and bearing his children was an integral part of that role. Perhaps the most important part. In other circumstances, in another time, perhaps I could have convinced him that what he proposed was beyond what I could stand. But as it was, I couldn't hope to escape the full obligations of a cognate. The stakes were too high.

It was, as it had always been, far bigger than me.

And now I knew what it would take for Dorian to deliberately change me. Because there was no way I could ever agree to this.

I should stay silent, I knew. Even objecting was dangerous. I could feel it, but I couldn't hold my peace. Not about this. It was too important and too horrifying.

"You expect me to…" I pointed from him to me and back, unable to even say it. "With you."

"To bear my children," he said. "Yes, Cora, I do."

"So I'm breeding stock," I said. "I'm supposed to make more of you. More monsters. God, Dorian, don't you see what's wrong with that? You say that the other agnates view humans as cattle. You think a...a brood-mare is any better? You think that I'm here to make babies for you, babies who will all grow up to be serial killers!"

"No," he said quietly. "That is what my research is for. They will not have to kill because they will find cognates, perhaps with their very first feeding. They won't have to continue the cycle of death. We can all break free."

"One in one hundred, Dorian," I said. "Those were my odds of survival. *That* is supposed to break the cycle? How?"

His jaw tightened for an instant. "It's only the first step. At first, our research could only eliminate half of those who wouldn't survive, then it could screen out ninety percent—by the time you came, ninety-nine. Soon, we'll be able to eliminate ninety-nine point nine, and one in ten will make it. And the other nine, like you, will chose to take the chance rather than face certain death. How is that not a good thing?"

"Because the other nine will still die, even then," I said. "And if it was my child who took that life, my heart would break."

"What if your human child became a doctor who only worked on the most lethal cases?" he returned. "What if he developed a procedure that would save some who would otherwise die, but would hasten the death of the remainder?"

I shook my head. "It's not the same. You forget that I lay there, on that couch, and I could feel…I could feel everything. I have a better idea of what you are than you think, and I can't have that for my children." I closed my eyes. "I can't even believe I'm talking about this. Children. Like it might be real. Like it could happen. I'm not having babies with anybody right now. Not you, not anyone."

"You don't have to," he said. "Not yet. Ten years is a very long time for someone as young as you."

Ten years. Ten years with him. In that time, he could persuade me of almost anything, without even meaning to do so. Black was white, good was evil. Ten years as his cognate—I couldn't even imagine how much of myself could be eroded in that time, by the force of his will.

He wouldn't have to bend my mind at that point. It would already be bent to him.

I thought of the preparations for the party that were taking place just beyond the door to the study. The celebration of my arrival, of a once-human to put in the hole carved out for me so long ago—mate, blood-giver, and mother.

I opened my eyes.

"No," I said aloud.

"What?" His gaze raked across my face. I could feel the force of his will around me, and he seemed to grow, tendrils of darkness extending out from him.

But I couldn't sit back while he shaped me, slowly, and pretended that he'd done nothing. I'd been too afraid of what he might do to defy him before. Yet he might as well have scrambled my brain already if I was too frightened to resist him. I had to stop this, if I could, before it was too late.

And I had to find out exactly how much of myself was at risk, to what measures he would go to force my obedience when the stakes were so high.

What if he makes you want to stay, want to have his children? a voice whispered inside my head. *What if he messes with your mind and then makes you happy about the change?*

I took a breath.

"No," I repeated. My voice was high and clear, each word carefully chosen. "No. I won't be introduced tonight. I can't do it. And if it means being the mother to your children, I'm not going to be your cognate."

"It's not something you can choose," he said, sounding more weary than angry as he stood.

I shook my head, backing toward the door. "It has to be. The world is full of choices. Maybe…maybe I'll go crazy without you. But I'll just have to, because even that's better than the alternative."

He stepped toward me, the power gathering around him. "The time for choices was the night you arrived here. If I had told you all this, then, would it have made a difference?"

I thought of the madness that had come over me that night, the recklessness, my willingness to let everything go—and my desperation to live. And I couldn't say for certain that it would have.

Dorian started to reach out. I jerked back out of his reach because I knew what would happen if he touched me. I could feel his influence over me, almost palpable, calling me to him, but I hardened myself against it.

"I won't stay, Dorian. I won't be a part of this."

"The guests will be arriving in less than two hours." His mouth was hard, his pale skin like marble, and the darkness pulsed around him, reaching outward, reaching for me. There was nothing human about him now, nothing tender in his pale, flat eyes, nothing for me to hang my hope on as he closed the space between us. "Whether you like it or not, you are a part of this world now. You have a role to fulfill. A role you *must* fulfill."

A role as his cognate. My mind balked at the ludicrousness of it, but I could feel his influence washing around me, swallowing me in it, taking my will apart piece by piece. I struggled to hold onto my determination, but the harder I grasped for it, the faster it slipped away until only the memory remained.

He didn't even have to touch me. My will dissolved at his merest desire.

I had my answer. I knew now what he'd do, what he'd take. I had been selected for a role, and he would not permit me to do less than fulfill it completely, because it was only in that role that he desired me.

And my heart ached with the weight of that knowledge.

Dorian stopped a foot away. He raised his hand and brushed my cheek softly, and in spite of everything, I leaned into his touch, even though I hated myself for it.

"I am sorry, Cora," he said. "This is greater than both of us."

And the remnants of my resistance were gone with that, torn from my mind, and I knew I would do whatever he asked of me. I blinked back tears.

"Stay. It is only one night," he said gently.

He didn't need to demand any longer. I couldn't refuse him because he'd taken that away from me. But it wasn't just one night—it was the first night, the first of thousands that would lead me, one step at a time, where I didn't want to go.

"You know I have to," I said. "You've made me. And you don't even understand that there is anything wrong with that."

Dorian pulled me against his chest then, and my body yielded to his, as it must.

He spoke into my hair. "You still don't understand what's at stake, Cora. You might think that you do, but you can't. Not yet. I hope you'll forgive me when you do."

"Will I have a choice?" I whispered.

He loosened his hold and stepped away, his eyes shadowed with a grief I couldn't name.

"Yes," he said. "I promise. This is going to be a difficult night for you. I can't help that. This is a tradition that I must honor even as I insist that you honor it. But I want you to listen to me closely, and keep these words in mind no matter what you see tonight."

A chill went up my spine, and I started to speak, but he placed a finger across my lips. I swayed slightly at the touch, and he looked down at me with such intensity that I swallowed.

"Just listen, Cora, and believe. This is the one event

in society to which an invitation must be, by rights, extended to all. And it is the only invitation that it is a deadly insult to refuse without just cause. There will be many in this house who have never before been allowed across this threshold and, if I have my way, never will again. We're not all the same any more than humans are all the same. No matter what you see, know that I am not them."

I nodded mutely.

The tension in his voice was palpable. "You won't be the only cognate, either. Many others will be in attendance with their agnates. But what they have is not necessarily what we will have. Don't be afraid, Cora. You know in your heart what I am. And what I am not."

But do I? I wondered. *Do I really?*

He stepped back, grasping me by the shoulders at arm's length. "Go finish getting dressed. I'll come for you when it is time to descend. I won't be able to stand beside you all evening, but you fled from the djinn and survived. You're stronger than you give yourself credit for. You can do this."

I laughed in my bitterness, the sound tearing at my throat. "I must. You've made me."

He nodded, accepting the accusation with sadness in his eyes that changed nothing.

I closed my eyes as he planted a chaste kiss on my cheek. Then I left the study. Obediently.

I had no alternative.

"There you are, Cora!" said Jane when I entered the bedroom. She glanced at the watch on her wrist.

"Still plenty of time."

She sent me to the bathroom, then herded me into the dressing room again, and I stood, dazed, as she dressed me, made repairs to my makeup and hair, and fussed over my perfume. I put on the heels that she gave me and stood for the necklace, earrings, and bracelet to be added.

Why shouldn't I be draped in Dorian's clothes, Dorian's jewels? After all, I was his possession as well.

"Take a look, madam," Worth said, pulling me over to a three-angled, floor length mirror.

I stared at the creature, and it stared back at me. I knew it was me, and yet I couldn't make a connection to the image in the mirror. She looked gorgeous, waiflike, and far too fragile to be real. She looked like she could belong to Dorian Thorne. She certainly didn't belong to me.

"Thank you," I said, and the lips of the figure moved, too. I looked away, unable to meet her eyes anymore.

Worth led me back into the bedroom and pushed a chair out for me. I sat, and she pulled her phone from her pocket. She typed something rapidly and then smiled at me, sympathy in her eyes. "I ordered water for you, madam. You seem somewhat out of sorts."

Perhaps she would understand. If anyone could. "I want what he wants, Worth," I said hopelessly. "Even when I don't."

"He is a good master, Cora," she said earnestly. "You're lucky to have him. All cognates are wanted, as much as they want their agnates. They must be. But his caring goes deeper than that."

I shook my head, unsure if I believed it, unsure if it made any difference if it were true.

There was a knock on the door then, and Jane went to answer it, returning with a sweat-beaded carafe and a crystal glass. She poured me a glass, and I drank it. The cold water did a little to clear my head.

"Thanks," I said.

I remembered suddenly and grabbed the chartreuse purse from the day before. I pulled out the pack of birth control pills.

Did I believe? Dared I believe?

The faint headache I'd had since yesterday had faded. I turned my wrist to reveal the teardrop-shaped bond mark. My fingers curled into a fist, almost of their own volition, and I put the pills back.

The next knock was Dorian. He had changed since I had seen him last and was now dressed in a white tie and tail suit. Not a hair was out of place. It made me hurt to look at him.

His gaze raked over my body, a light of desire burning deep in his eyes.

"Exquisite," he said succinctly. "Are you ready?"

I nodded and stood, passing him carefully without touching as I went through the doorway onto the mezzanine. I could hear the chatter of the guests below and the quiet playing of a small orchestra. He offered me his arm. I shrank away, but the force of his personality overwhelmed me and I took it despite myself. He guided me to the top of the stairs.

"Remember, Cora," he said, capturing me in his

gaze. "We are not all the same."

We descended to the salon, side-by-side, to meet the room full of vampires.

The story continues in…

BLOOD RITES

Cora's Choice – Book 4
AETHEREAL BONDS

Want to read the first chapter right now? Sign up for the newsletter at AetherealBonds.com to get exclusive access—for free! Get free content and release updates.

Blood-bonded to the billionaire vampire Dorian Thorne, Cora Shaw enters a world of unimagined sensuality—and unimagined danger. With the hold he has over her, he can exert absolute control over her body and mind, even to the point of erasing her completely.

And Dorian has already shown a willingness to use his power to force her to do his will.

Cora is determined to find a way out of her bond, no matter what the price. But even as she seeks an escape, she wonders if she can really let him go….

ABOUT THE AUTHOR

V. M. Black is the creator of Aethereal Bonds, a sensual paranormal romance urban fantasy series that takes vampires, shifters, and faes where they've never been before. You can find her on AetherealBonds.com. Visit to connect through her mailing list and various social media platforms across the web.

She's a proud geek who lives near Washington, D.C., with her family, and she loves fantasy, romance, science fiction, and historical fiction.

All of her books are available in a number of digital formats. Don't have an e-reader? No problem! You can download free reading apps made by every major retailer from your phone or tablet's app store and carry your books with you wherever you go.